The Way It Is

The Way It Is

Kareem

www.urbanbooks.net

Urban Books, LLC
97 N18th Street
Wyandanch, NY 11798

ISBN 13: 978-1-62286-975-6
ISBN 10: 1-62286-975-3

First Mass Market Printing February 2016
Printed in the United States of America

10 9 8 7 6 5 4 3 2 1

Distributed by Kensington Publishing Corp.
Submit orders to:
Customer Service
400 Hahn Road
Westminster, MD 21157-4627
Phone: 1-800-733-3000
Fax: 1-800-659-2436

1

You Done Bumped Your Head

"*Ese muchacho* is gonna learn the hard way to respect his elders." The elderly Hispanic man uttered this to himself as he watched Derrick's car slowly passing by like it was a hearse in a funeral procession. The young man was slumped down in the driver's seat and leaning sideways. He was sitting so low in his ride that only his dark blue New York Yankees baseball cap could be seen. His music, rapper Jay-Z's "Hard Knock Life," was blasting hard and outrageously loud, sending shockwaves through the neighborhood.

It was Sunday morning and considered blatantly disrespectful by the elders and the religious communities for anyone to be blasting music as loud as Derrick's speakers were while church service was being conducted. Derrick, however, didn't give a damn. He looked over at the elderly Hispanic man and saw him fixing his face in an agitated fashion. The elderly man shook his head in the negative at Derrick's ill demeanor. Instead of Derrick refraining from interfering with the peace of the elderly man and church service that was being held at the church on the corner of the neighborhood, he gave the elderly man his middle finger and turned his music up even louder.

"Boy, turn that music down. Haven't you any respect?" the elderly man yelled.

"Won't you put some teeth in your mutha-fuckin' mouth?" Derrick shot back. *Fuckin' old folks always thinking a nigga gotta give them some respect. I ain't gotta do a damn thing. Fuck them!*

The elderly Hispanic man grabbed his cane, got up from his chair on his porch, and went inside his house. "I am old enough to be the young man's *padre*, but he disrespects me like I'm someone his age. Heavenly Father, forgive him."

Derrick continued moving through the hood. He was smoking on some of the greenest and most potent weed on the west side of Charlotte, North Carolina, where there were more young black men roaming the hood without fathers in their lives than there were police patrolling the streets where the young men hustled. Derrick was one of them: a young man, eighteen years old to be exact, without a father figure in his life. He had just graduated the previous year from high school, and had only one thing on his mind: getting money. He certainly had reasons.

He took a left on Lanordo Street and parked in the lot of an apartment that rested right at the corner of Lanordo and Bivens Streets. He killed his engine and exited his candy apple red chromed-out old-school Chevy Impala. He was wearing a white khaki polo shirt, blue jeans by Calvin Klein, and all-white Air Force Ones. Derrick's jeans were so oversized that when he walked they fell below his buttocks. Had he been in a prison environment wearing his pants in such a manner, some male looking for a young man to become his prison bitch would walk up to him without warning and touch him on his ass cheeks in hopes of having an intimate affair. Or, worse, rape him!

He took a deep drag from his marijuana cigarette, released the smoke from his nostrils after holding it in a few seconds, then said with both his hands lifted skyward, "The world is mines!"

His little eleven-year-old brother, Mike-Mike, was sitting on the front steps of their apartment, playing with his basketball. "Who are you now, Scarface?" his little brother asked.

4
KareemKareem

"Damn right. I'm Tony muthafuckin' Montana!"

"Derrick, boy, you high. Betta not let Momma see—"

Before Mike-Mike could finish his sentence, their mother came out of their apartment. She marched toward Derrick. "I know you ain't smoking a blunt out here in my yard, Derrick." She reached for it. Although high as the sky, he managed to dodge her attempt. "You done bumped your head for real. You know I don't pl—"

"I know, I know, Momma. You don't play that," he said, cutting her off and tossing the blunt somewhere onto the lawn. "I really don't see what the fuss is all about though. It's just weed."

Arms folded, she repeated, "Just weed?"

"Yeah, Momma, just weed. A natural herb from the earth."

"I wouldn't give a fat baby's backside if it was only an Indian's peace pipe. You find somewhere else to puff on it! That stuff ain't doing nothing but killing your brain cells."

"A'ight then, whatever. If I wanted to hear a sermon I would have gone to church," he muttered.

"What you say? I promise you, boy, I'll knock your teeth straight down your damn throat."

"Yeah, and I'll forget all about you, too," Derrick uttered to himself. "This woman needs a man in her life. Every day she finds something to trip about," he said under his breath, walking toward Mike-Mike. He put his open palm on top of his little brother's forehead and slightly pushed it back. "What's up, knucklehead?"

"Nothing," replied Mike-Mike. "Just practicing my skills. I got a mean crossover; look." Mike-Mike started dribbling his basketball around and in and out of his legs. "Try to take the ball from me, Derrick."

Derrick positioned himself to take the ball but, when he reached for it, his little brother did a crossover move on him so smooth and sweet that Derrick nearly broke his ankle in his attempt to take the ball. "Okay, li'l bruh. I see you got mad skills."

"Told you."

"Keep it up and you might end up in the NBA one day."

"Might?"

"You've gotta work hard, also on your schoolwork. What your report card look like anyway?"

"I passed to the next grade. Didn't I, Momma?" Their mother was still standing there with her arms folded. Before she could reply, Mike-Mike added, "You know my birthday's tomorrow."

"And?"

"And you promised me that you were gonna buy me some Air Force Ones. The all-white ones like yours."

"Well, I lied. Now what?"

Mike-Mike sucked his teeth and made his sad face. "C'mon now, Derrick, you promised me that—"

"Have I ever made a promise to you that I didn't keep?" Derrick said, cutting him off.

"No, but you just said that you lied about getting me those Air Force Ones."

"Boy, you know I got you." Derrick then hit his little brother hard in his upper left arm.

"Ouchhh! Man, that hurt."

"Shut up and take it like a man. What I tell you about being all soft?"

Derrick's mother hit him hard in his chest. "And what I tell you about hitting him like that? He's a kid, not a punching bag."

"So what? That doesn't mean he gotta be soft. I don't want no soft, sugar-filled brother."

"Hitting him, Derrick, is not gonna make him hard or manly."

"With all due respect, Momma, how do you know? You're not a man."

"And you not his daddy. For your information, I don't have to be a man to know what one acts like. If you wanna do something, try being a positive example for him to follow. Now let me see you inside the house. I got a bone to pick with you."

Derrick immediately knew that something had to be wrong. Anytime his mother didn't want to talk to him about something in the presence of Mike-Mike, it was serious.

The north side of Charlotte bred niggas who would bust a nigga's bubble for simply looking at a gangsta the wrong way. God forbid a nigga say the wrong thing out of his mouth. On that side of town, before the sun could grace the sky fully with its presence, a meeting was being conducted. Fat Jerome, a big-time drug dealer, had ordered two of his most ruthless hit men to meet him at a gambling house off Fifteenth Street and Davison Avenue. The two hitmen were Tye-Tye and Rasco. Tye-Tye was known for cutting dudes' throats and leaving 'em in the woods to bleed to death. And Rasco was known for putting his 9 mm Glock in his enemy's mouth and pulling the trigger. The two of them only did jobs for Fat Jerome. They made Fat Jerome one of the most feared drug dealers to work for.

"Fellas, I requested this meeting because I got a li'l problem on the west side with an individual

I gave some coke to on consignment. I really didn't want to fuck with the kid, but Veronda convinced me."

"You talking 'bout li'l fine-ass Veronda, the ex-stripper who used to run li'l errands and shit for us, right?" asked Tye-Tye.

"Right. She fucks with the guy and asked me to front him something on her name. Since the bitch cool and shit, I hit the li'l nigga off with a whole kilo."

"A kilo? Damn, Fat Jerome, you ain't never gave me a kilo of coke to hustle," interjected Rasco, scratching his arm like a junkie fiending for drugs.

His outburst made Fat Jerome mad. But because of a flight he had to catch, he kept his anger under control. "Cut the bullshit. You're a killa, not a damn drug dealer."

"Yeah, but—"

"Just play your position, dawg. You don't see the lungs in your body trying to do what your kidneys are responsible for doing, do you?"

"I'm just saying—"

"Nah, answer my question."

Rasco looked at Tye-Tye who kept his eyes on Fat Jerome. "You right, dawg," said Rasco. "You right."

"Precisely. Besides, whether I give you coke to hustle or not, I still take care of you and Tye, don't I?"

"Fat Jerome, you take good care of us, trust me," interjected Tye-Tye. Tye-Tye didn't know why Rasco would fix his mouth to say what he said to Fat Jerome, because Fat Jerome had both of them eating good. In Tye-Tye's eyes there was no need to complain.

"Man, I was just throwing that out there, that's all," said Rasco. "No offense intended," he lied. Truth was, he not only wanted to do hits, he wanted to step his game up and become his own boss so that he could do as he pleased, including drugs if he wanted to.

"Do that shit on your own time. I got a fuckin' flight to catch," said Fat Jerome, trying to keep his anger on ice and chill. He hated being interrupted, especially for something frivolous, or for something that could have waited to be brought up some other time. He sighed, and then continued.

"Now, that young cat I was telling y'all about, I was hitting him off good with coke, and the nigga never came up short with my cheese 'til here recently. I shot him a block last month and haven't heard from him since."

"The nigga hasn't called you or nothing?" asked Tye-Tye.

"He hasn't done shit. In fact, I tried his and Veronda's cell phone numbers. Both of their numbers changed. And Veronda ain't living at the same address she was living at prior to this shit."

"So I guess this young nigga call himself not paying you then, huh?" asked Tye.

"Precisely. Which means we gotta straight punish his ass. If the nigga feels like his balls are that big to fuck me, then it's time to show him how we crack balls that big."

Rasco cracked his knuckles. "Oh, fo'sho', my nigga."

Fat Jerome threw him the keys to his Hummer, and tossed him a small Ziploc bag full of chronic. "Put that underneath my driver's side seat." While Rasco went to do so, Fat Jerome motioned with his head for Tye-Tye to lag behind. When Rasco was clearly out of sight, Fat Jerome said to Tye-Tye, "Rasco's loyalty is questionable, and we can't have that. Plus, I heard from a reliable source that the nigga done started smoking crack. This, you and I both know, is a violation in our crew." One of Fat Jerome's rules for those of his Cash Money Clique was "no getting high." No getting high off their supply or anyone else's. Fat

Jerome believed that drugs like coke and heroin clouded a street soldier's vision. So, drug use was strictly prohibited.

"Nah, we don't do that shit. That's for the junkies. But is this shit true, though?" Tye-Tye shot back.

"It's true. And remember when my dope house in Matthews, North Carolina, got robbed?"

"Yeah, I remember you telling me about that shit," Tye-Tye responded, with his nose spread and a mean street grit on his face.

"Word is, his ass is the one who set that shit up. The nigga who told me said that Rasco came to him first and asked him if he wanted to make some fast cash. He told the dude what was up, but when the dude found out that Rasco wanted him to rob a spot that belonged to me, he refused. This same nigga smoke weed laced with crack. He said he and Rasco done smoked that shit numerous times together."

"So why is this coming to the surface now, Fat Jerome? Matter of fact, where is this nigga who told you all this?"

"I heard the nigga got popped coming back from Miami somewhere. His name was Short-Arm."

"I know that nigga. He has been missing about a good-ass seven or eight months."

"Precisely. The reason I didn't say anything is because I wanted to give Rasco the benefit of the doubt. But when the nigga screamed just a moment ago about me not ever giving him any crack to sell, he made me fuckin' angry. He's a nigga we no longer need, therefore, see his ass, because, Tye, little violations left uncheck leads to big ones. Rasco is a snake. And some snakes don't rattle. That's what makes them so deadly."

"I'll holler at him ASAP," replied Tye-Tye.

"Precisely. And do it the thug way," said Fat Jerome as the two of them parted company.

Fat Jerome was a thirty-five-year-old drug dealer who believed in unity. He hated dishonest, disloyal street soldiers. He knew that a house divided couldn't stand. Therefore, weak links had to be eliminated regardless of the major love one might have for that weak link. He loved Rasco, because it was Rasco who saved his ass from catching a sexually transmitted disease.

At the time, he didn't know Rasco, nor did Rasco know him. Rasco had only heard of Fat Jerome as a dude whose name was ringing all over the Queen City for being deep in the game. While at a strip club one night, though, Rasco saw this real big, fat-ass dude—six foot three and every bit of 300 pounds—standing in front of the stage that the strippers were doing their dances on. The fat dude was light skinned with long dreadlocks that hung far down his back just above his Gucci belt. On his wrist was a diamond bezel platinum Rolex watch that sparkled every time lights from the club reflected off of it. In the fat man's hands were stacks of cash that he handed out to the strippers who twirled booty and pussy in his face.

One of the girls who stripped and danced before the fat man was a chick Rasco knew well. Her name was Jessica, a white chick with a fat ass who had death on her pussy. Rasco knew her from high school. She had syphilis, the same STD that put gangster and mob boss Al Capone's dick in the dirt. Before Jessica could drop to her knees to give the fat man some head, Rasco interrupted, "Yo, big man, trust me, you don't want this bitch sucking your dick. The bitch got syphilis."

The fat man looked at Rasco. "Yo, who the fuck are you and how did you get in here?" he questioned, realizing Rasco had entered the VIP room uninvited.

"I know the club owner, dawg. Regardless of that, this here bitch got death on her pussy. Ain't that fuckin' right, Jessica?"

"Nigga, you lying like the devil," she shot back, getting up from her knees.

"I'm lying?" Rasco repeated. He then grabbed her by the back of her hair. "Bitch, if I'm lying then this lying-ass nigga 'bout to blow your brains out 'cause you know your pussy got death on it." He slipped his 9 mm out from his waist and positioned it at her head.

"Hold on. Hold on, yo. Put your gun away, bro, and let the ho go," the fat man ordered.

Rasco pushed her head hard toward the door, and kicked her in her ass. "Stankin'-ass bitch! You know that pussy between your legs would send a nigga to his grave. I hate y'all kind of bitches."

"You just a hater," she shouted, before storming out of VIP and slamming the door behind her.

Rasco put his gun away and looked at the fat man. "Excuse me, big man, for the interruption, but that bitch dirty. You look like a cool dude, so I just wanted to warn you."

"Dayum, man, for a minute I didn't know what the fuck was going on. I appreciate you, though, shit. By the way, I'm Fat Jerome."

"Nice to meet you, Fat Jerome. If you ever need a true soldier in your corner, I'm available," Rasco assured him. Fat Jerome had a lot of soldiers who rolled with him. He honestly didn't need any more. However, there was *something about this five foot eleven dark-skinned, slim soldier, Rasco, that Fat Jerome liked. It was the fact that Rasco had just aggressively saved his life and was extremely bold about it. That was enough to make Rasco a part of his moneymaking team. Since Rasco was aggressive and wasn't afraid to use a gun, Fat Jerome linked him up with Tye-Tye and the both of them were used as hit men.*

All Fat Jerome wanted any soldier in his crew to do was simply play their position and the family would continue to get money. He didn't want killers in his crew selling drugs, because all his killers had quick tempers. No one with a quick temper and short fuse would make a good drug dealer, because the very moment someone came up short with cash, those quick-tempered killers would have bodies all over Queen City.

Being a drug dealer meant compromising sometimes. So, Fat Jerome did his best to keep his soldiers in their rightful place. Rasco wanted to evolve though. When he secretly robbed one of his boss man's drug houses, as well as started secretly smoking crack, and now a sudden outburst at an important meeting, he had proven himself to be a problem. A problem that Tye-Tye was now ordered to solve.

***

Derrick followed his mother into her bedroom and closed the door behind him. His mother went straight to her closest and retrieved a large brown paper bag. She tossed it onto her bed. Derrick immediately knew what it contained.

"What in the hell have I told you about bringing this garbage where we lay our heads, huh, Derrick? This stuff was sitting right out on my living room sofa where Mike-Mike could have very well gotten to it."

"Momma, I'm sorry. I forg—"

"I don't want to hear you forgot. You know, if those housing authority folks were to come and do an unexpected inspection of our apartment and find that garbage in here, what's gonna happen?"

Derrick inhaled and exhaled hard. "I promise you, Momma, it won't happen again."

"Don't make promises you don't intend to keep. You can't even manage to keep your mind clear enough to think right. Look at you, you stay high on that weed stuff, twenty-four/seven. You swore up and down when you graduated a year ago that you were either going to the military or enrolling in barber college. You have done neither. Instead, you come in every night with large amounts of money you made off of selling that crack-cocaine garbage. You try spoiling

Mike-Mike with that drug money by buying him things. But I work hard every day to ensure that we have something—"

"Something like what, Momma? A government apartment to stay in?" Derrick said, cutting her off. "I'm sick and tired of the hood. All I've ever known is the hood. That's all my little brother knows as well. If we continue staying here, both me and my brother will do nothing but eventually become products of our environment. Yes, I was gonna go in the military, but since President Bush took office, the majority of the young males entering the military get deployed to Iraq, and are coming home in body bags. So I had to rethink going into the military. Barber school, well, I still might pursue that."

"I can't tell."

"You can't tell, Momma, because you're too busy pointing out the wrong that I do, without first seeing what it is I'm trying to accomplish."

Derrick was sick and tired of what living in the hood reminded him of, as well as how it made him feel on a constant basis. Living in the hood reminded him daily that he, his mother, and his little brother, Mike-Mike, were poor. As a result of their poverty, they had to be assisted by a government that Derrick believed had

never had poor people's best interests at heart.
Especially poor black people. As far as Derrick
was concerned, the government, through its
welfare programs, caused many single mothers
to sit around idle and wait for a support check
every month. And even though Derrick's mother
worked, she had to do so undercover, without
the government knowing about it, because if she
made more money on her job than the government allowed, the government would terminate
her welfare benefits in a hurry. In addition,
Derrick hated the fact that while his father was
alive, his father was not allowed by the government to stay with them at their apartment as
long as his mother was being assisted by welfare.
That, Derrick believed, affected their family's
stability. He felt that instead of the government
disallowing his father to stay with them, the
government should have promoted it for
the purpose of their family staying together.

His father was sick with a chronic drug addic-
tion. Heroin was his father's drug of choice,
only because his father was unable to cope with
some tragedies he witnessed while serving in
the United States Marines. His father suffered
from post-traumatic stress disorder. After his
failed attempt at receiving veterans benefits,
his heroin use increased. Living in the hood

reminded young Derrick of all of this, and more. All he wanted was just to get the hell up out of such; if not for his sake, for his little brother and their mother's. If only he could get his mother to understand this.

"Listen here, young man, I don't care what you are trying to accomplish," said Derrick's mother, getting directly up in his face. "You are my child, and I refuse to see you on the damn six o'clock news somewhere. Look at what happened to your father."

"Momma, you don't have to keep reminding me about what happened to my daddy. I know he was found in an alley with a needle in his arm. Besides, I'm not on drugs."

"You think you have to be on drugs to be a victim of what drugs can do, Derrick? If so, then who's being naive?"

Derrick sucked his teeth, placed his brown paper bag full of ready-to-sell cocaine underneath his armpit, and was about to leave.

"Don't you walk away from me when I'm talking to you, Derrick," his mother shouted.

Derrick had tears in his eyes. He hated to be reminded of his father's absence. Even though he was only an eight-year-old kid when his father died, he still remembered his father sitting him on his lap, telling him that he loved him, and kissing him on his forehead, which always made him feel good.

"Momma, I'm just doing what I gotta do to help us get out the hood. Why can't you just accept that?"

"'Cause you still a kid, that's why."

"Momma, I'm almost nineteen."

"I wouldn't care if you were almost a hundred. You'll never be older than me. Now, I apologize for reminding you of your father. But listen here, those streets and those drugs will take you under. I see it every day. Every day on the news some mother is crying because her child has gotten shot down either from gang violence, or from just being a part of the drug game. Do you know what it means to a mother to lose a child? I think not because you're not one."

"But, Momma—"

"No, don't 'but, Momma' me! That drug game, boy, is nothing but one gigantic mirage that's full of illusions. It all leads down the same path, a one-way street to destruction with no fork in the road."

Derrick sighed. *Here she go with the preachin' again.* "You right, Momma."

"No, I don't need you to affirm whether I'm right or wrong. I need for you to clean your act up, and not bring that garbage back into our house."

"You mean this government apartment?"

"Whatever. You ought to be thankful you got a roof over your head. Some people ain't got that. If you had it your way, you, me, and Mike-Mike would be sleeping out in the streets."

"We would be sleepin' out in the streets? Why would you say that, when I'm doing everything in my power to help get us into our own home, Momma?"

"You doing everything but the right thing. 'Cause, like I said, if those housing authority folks were to do an unexpected inspection here, ain't no tellin' what they would find illegal of yours. Those drugs in that paper bag underneath your arm, anybody could have spotted it in our living room. But you stay so high off of that weed you constantly smoke that you don't even know where you be placing that stuff. All I'm telling you is don't bring that stuff back in here. Derrick, I mean that! Now get it out of here!"

Derrick's mother was a strict, no-nonsense woman. She wanted the best for both of her sons. But raising two boys wasn't easy at all. She was a forty-seven-year-old high school dropout whose only income was a government check once a month, and the pay she received weekly from working for an elderly retired doctor as a housekeeper. Every dime she earned went toward purchasing food and clothing, paying her car off, and buying other little things necessary for her, Mike-Mike, and Derrick. Derrick often refused to let her buy him anything. After he started hustling coke, he insisted on purchasing things for her and Mike-Mike. The few times Derrick tried giving his mother large amounts of cash, she refused to accept it. She told him she didn't accept dirty money.

"There is no such thing as dirty money," Derrick always responded. But in his mother's eyes, money earned the illegal way was money she didn't want to spend, let alone have in her possession.

"Well, Momma, the money you make without the government knowing about it, what kind of money is that? Is it legal, or illegal?" Derrick once asked his mother.

"It's money I earn the honest way. I just don't report it because the government will raise my rent."

Derrick knew the government would indeed raise his mother's rent if she reported that she was working and the job was paying her pretty nicely. Still, Derrick laughed hard at her reply. "Momma, you got game."

"Whateva."

2

I Don't Give A Fuck About Fat Jerome

Derrick left his mother's apartment, jumped into his ride, and hit the highway. He did so with the express intent of never bringing cocaine into his mother's place again. He knew she would verbally spank his ass for his carelessness of leaving his moneymaking product out as he did. For that, he felt somewhat ashamed. He pulled up at his girlfriend Veronda's crib. He exited his car with his brown paper bag underneath his armpit. He hit the doorbell and after waiting a minute or two, Veronda answered.

"Hey, baby. I didn't know you were coming over," she said, standing before him in her white tee and tight booty shorts.

"Neither did I, this early," he responded, sidestepping her to enter into her living room. Usually he would greet her with a kiss, but his mother checking him for slipping had him a little discombobulated.

"My mom's fuckin' trippin'," he continued.

"'Bout what?"

"'Bout this." Derrick tossed her the brown paper bag.

Veronda caught it and took a peek inside. "Hell, no wonder, boo. You know damn well your mom don't play with you selling drugs."

"I fucked up and left the shit lying out on the sofa in her living room."

"That's even worse. I know that li'l pretty mother of yours pitched a fit."

"She did everything but shoot my ass."

"Shit, if she had a gun I'm sure she would've," replied Veronda, laughing.

"Threatened to knock my teeth down my throat and everything."

"You gon' run your mother crazy, Derrick, I swear."

"Not on purpose, Veronda. Look, all I'm trying to do is fuckin' get us out the damn hood."

"You will eventually, baby. Rome wasn't built in a night. Neither were the Egyptian pyramids."

"I know that."

"Slow down then," she said, caressing his face with her hand.

"I can't fuckin' move at a snail's pace on this one. It's now or never. 'Cause the hood I stay in ain't got nothing but a bunch of fuckin' drug dealers, robbers, and pimps in there. Every day my little brother walks home from school and he has to witness this shit. I know, because I had to witness it too when I was his age. Now look at what I've become: a damn drug dealer. Someone I said I would never become. Now ain't that a bitch?"

"Life's a bitch, depending on how you dress her. Like I said, baby boy, in time you will have what it is you seek. That is, if you don't get careless and start moving too fast."

"I'm just tired of this hood bullshit."

"I can dig it, Derrick. Besides, where the hell you think I'm from? I'm just saying take it slow."

"Speaking of the hood, though, you ever wonder why they never call the projects a neighborhood? You know, like rich people stay in a neighborhood, but the poor, the hood."

"I've never really given it any thought," replied Veronda. "Why you think it's like that?"

"I think it's like that because poor people, particularly black poor people, we always getting the 'ass end' of every damn thing! They remove 'neighbor' and give us 'hood.' A fuckin' hood is

defined as something that goes over one's head.
This shit is a trip."

"Boy, you too much. You always thinking and
coming up with something."

"Naw, I'm just keeping it real, Veronda. I'm
just keepin' it fuckin' real."

"You definitely got a point, though. But peep
this. You know you also got your hands full with
this Fat Jerome thang, right?"

"Veronda, for real for real, I don't give a fuck
about Fat Jerome, or the li'l niggas who work for
that muthafucka!"

"I know but—"

"But what? Shit, ain't nothing to discuss about
that fat muthafucka. After what you told me he
did to you, I had a right to take his coke. The
pig's lucky I didn't take his life."

"Boo, don't talk like that."

"What, you getting soft on me, Veronda?"

"No."

"That fat nigga took you over to his place,
got you pissy drunk and when you awoke you
discovered that the fat bitch had sodomized you.
I understand you didn't want to break the G code
of the streets, but for real for real you should
have gone and taken out a warrant on his ass."

"He would have only gotten out; then my life
really would have been in danger. See, Derrick,

I've been knowing Fat for a while. I know what he is capable of doing. Well, not him, but the li'l goons who run with him, especially Rasco and Tye-Tye. They'll do anything for him, no bullshit."

"Them niggas aren't the only ones who'll hurt something," Derrick shot back.

"That's not what I'm indicating. All I'm saying is Fat Jerome is not gonna sit around idly, knowing someone has failed to pay him, and do nothing."

"Look, the fact remains the nigga was wrong for what he did to you. Doing that to you was like him doing it to me. Shit, he knew you were my girl when he did it. That's like me laughing and grinning in his face daily, then, when he turns his back, I snatch the chick he care about and screw her. Now, how would that look, and he and I supposed to be business associates? I never once failed to pay him. I only decided not to give him shit after what you told me you suspected he did to you."

"Not suspected. The nigga did it to me," Veronda corrected him.

"Well, he fucked you, and I fucked him. Whatever he wants to do about it, we can do it. 'Cause, honestly, I don't give a fuck. Besides, is my .44 Desert Eagle still in your closet?"

"You know I'm afraid of guns, Derrick. So, if you placed it in my closet it's definitely still there."

"Good."

Derrick walked into Veronda's bedroom. He went straight to her closet while she placed the paper bag full of coke underneath her mattress. When Veronda looked up, she saw Derrick placing bullets in the clip of his gun.

"What you plan on doing with that, Derrick? I hope nothing stupid."

"I ain't gonna do anything stupid. I'm just strapping up because you're right; that fat muthafucka just might come looking for me. In the event that he does, all I can say is the big nigga betta come correct."

"Or?" asked Veronda.

"Or somebody will pay a severe fuckin' price."

Derrick wasn't a "hard as hell" street gangsta who thrived on looking for trouble. He was in the streets to stack paper, not to start problems. Derrick wasn't a punk either. He knew beyond a doubt that being soft in the game meant getting pushed around, or pushed over. Neither would happen if Derrick could help it. So, when he started selling drugs, one of the first things he did was purchase a gun. Guns were easy to come across in the hood, and damn near every hustler and bad boy had one. With Fat Jerome and his goons looking for him, Derrick figured it was time he carry his gun on him everywhere he went. He couldn't chance slipping, because slipping on Fat Jerome and his crew could equate to a death sentence, and Derrick wasn't ready to die.

It was 11:45 p.m., and Fat Jerome's two hit men, Tye-Tye and Rasco, moved through the west side searching with eagle eyes for their eighteen-year-old target.

"We've been riding and looking for this young nigga damn near all night, Tye-Tye. And everybody we've asked over here on the west side act like they don't know who this nigga is, man," said Rasco.

"Somebody knows who he is, we just gotta be patient. You know how them young cats are. They get out here in these streets and start hustling and making a li'l money and the first thing they want is a li'l attention on their asses," replied Tye-Tye, who had more than killing Derrick on his mind.

"Tell me 'bout it," Rasco said.

"So they go buy the biggest and the nicest car their drug money can buy. They gotta have all the jewelry and half of them carry money around in their pockets, like their pocket is a bank or something. These niggas stupid. Stupidity causes a nigga to slip sooner or later."

"You right about that, Tye. Stupidity is a muthafucka. You sho' right."

"I know I am. Not just that, though. The majority of the young cats you see hustling out here, when the cops roll down on them the first thing they do is start rattin' on their friends and shit."

"Yep," replied Rasco.

"I know ain't none of us out here perfect and shit, but if you gon' be a gangsta, be a gangsta. Rattin' to the cops about what goes on in the streets ain't cool at all."

"Naw, that rattin' shit ain't cool, dawg. That shit ain't cool at all."

"Neither is getting out of line with someone who puts money in your pocket and food on your table," Tye-Tye said.

When Tye-Tye said that, Rasco embraced silence a moment; then he said, "What you mean by that, Tye-Tye?"

Tye-Tye was too mad to explain himself. "Hold on a minute, I gotta take a leak." Tye-Tye pulled his car over to the side of a lonely dirt road surrounded by trees. "I'll be back." Tye-Tye got out the car, took a leak, and headed back to the car. Instead of heading back to the driver's side, he walked straight up to the passenger's side. He opened the door in a hurry, yanked Rasco out, and cut Rasco's throat from one end of his neck to the other. It happened so fast that Rasco didn't stand a fighting chance.

"You're a snake-ass nigga." Tye-Tye watched Rasco struggle for air. "Don't fight it, mutha-fucka, it's over, all fuckin' over. You talk too damn much."

To bite the hand that feeds you in the streets was a violation of the gangsta code of loyalty. For a nigga to have an unbridled tongue was damn near equally the same, especially when the unbridled tongue talked bullshit in the midst of the boss man conducting business.

Tye-Tye followed up on what his boss ordered him to do. He took Rasco's life like it was no problem, wiped his bloodstained weapon over Rasco's clothing, and left him on the side of the lonely dirt road. He then got back into his car as if nothing had happened and continued his search for Derrick.

3

Happy Birthday, Li'l Mike

Monday Afternoon

"Where you get all of that money from, bruh, if you don't work?" asked Mike-Mike, as he stepped into Derrick's bedroom.

He didn't hear Mike-Mike approach because his music was up loud. "Don't worry about all that. What I tell you about being so nosy, anyway?"

"I wasn't being nosy. You had your door cracked."

"Regardless, what you doing looking in here? Do you sleep in here?"

"No, but—"

"But nothing." His little brother was about to walk away. "Come here, and shut my door behind you." Mike-Mike did as Derrick ordered. "How did you like your li'l birthday present I bought you?" he asked. He turned the volume down on N.W.A.'s *Straight Outta Compton* CD.

"Which one?"

"The one around your neck." Derrick bought Mike-Mike a diamond-cut rope chain with a Nike medallion. Mike-Mike reached for it and held it by the medallion. "I love this chain, bruh; it's nice."

"You betta. I paid twelve hundred dollars for it."

"Twelve hundred dollars? That's more than the Air Force Ones you bought me."

"I know. Don't tell Momma, though, a'ight?"

"I won't. Why were you and Momma arguing yesterday?"

"That's between Momma and me. Everything's fine though."

"When you left, I saw Momma in her room on her knees, praying and crying. I even heard her say in her prayer, 'God, I'm putting my son in your hands.' Who was she talking about, bruh? Me or you?"

"Probably you, Mike-Mike."

"Me? What I do?"

"Nah, Momma mad at me right now. You really wanna know why?"

"Why?"

"Well, li'l bruh, since you twelve years old today, I can start sharing more things with you. Momma mad at me because I do illegal things to make my money."

"Like what?"

"Like things I shouldn't be doing, and betta never ever see you doing."

"Like selling drugs?"

"Something like that. But anyway, she hates that I do illegal things."

"Why you do those things, bruh, if you know that the things you're doing will hurt her?"

Derrick put away his cash. "I don't mean to hurt Momma. I love Momma. But I love also doing what I gotta do to try to help us get out the hood. Little bruh, I hate the hood. Ain't nothing in the hood but poverty and more poverty. If it kills me, I gotta do what I gotta do to help get us out of here."

"Momma said that by this time next year we gonna be moving into a house of our own."

"I can't wait 'til next year. I wanna see us in our own house in a matter of months. And that's exactly what's gonna happen if things line up with how I have planned them. Now, besides all that, your Air Force Ones look good on your feet. Thought I wasn't gonna get them for you, didn't you?"

"Not really. I know you always look out for me. 'Preciate it, too."

Derrick placed his hand on top of Mike-Mike's head. "No problem. I want you to have everything that I was deprived of when I was your age. And make no mistake about it, little bruh, I'll do whatever I have to do to see you with what you like."

Mike-Mike put his arms around Derrick's waist. He really loved his big brother. "Guess what Momma bought me for my birthday? Well, you probably already know."

"No, I don't. What she get you?"

"Guess."

"A new basketball?"

"Nope."

"A new video game?"

"Nope, got enough of those."

"What she getcha then?"

"A brand new computer."

"Yeahhh?"

"Yep, a laptop. She said that she wanted me to be more than a basketball player. She says she wants me to be a lawyer."

"What do you wanna be? 'Cause at the end of the day, it's gonna be up to you."

"I don't know. But I think I want to be more like you, someone who will do any- and everything to see his family in a better situation."

"I think you can do that being a lawyer, Mike-Mike. Now let's take a ride. I got one other present for you for your birthday."

"Another present?"

"Definitely. You gon' really enjoy this one."

"Oh, yeah, Momma told me to tell you to call her at work when you came in. She had to get to work early. That's why she wasn't here when you arrived."

"Okay. I'll call her from my cell phone. Let's go."

Derrick's car pulled up at Veronda's apartment. When Veronda came out, the first thing li'l Mike-Mike said was, "Ain't that your girlfriend, bruh?"

"You betta believe it," replied Derrick.

"Man, she's fine. I remember when you brought her to our house. She's fine."

"You think so?"

"Know so."

Veronda stepped to the driver's side of the car, wearing an all-black skintight, full-body skirt, with some all-black stiletto heels. She had the legs and calves of an Olympic marathon runner. Her hair was long and curly like she was mixed with Indian and black. Her skin was caramel and her eyes were a pretty hazel; any man would melt looking into them. Li'l Mike-Mike was instantly in love, just like Derrick was when he first saw her shaking her booty at a strip club.

"Hey, baby," she said, kissing Derrick on his lips. "What you up to?"

"Just hanging out with my li'l brother, Mike-Mike. Today is his birthday."

"Really?" replied Veronda, looking over at Mike-Mike.

"Yep."

"Happy birthday, li'l Mike," she said.

"Thank you," Mike-Mike replied, smiling.

"Baby, don't you got something for my li'l brother?" Derrick said, smiling and winking his eye.

"Sure do," she replied, then walked around to where Mike-Mike was. She kissed him right smack dead on his lips.

Mike-Mike's heart skipped a beat. He looked over at Derrick and smiled.

"Don't look at me," said Derrick. "She's the one who kissed you, not me. What you say to a kiss like that?"

Mike-Mike shrugged his shoulders. "I don't know."

"You say, 'Can I please get another one?'"

Mike-Mike looked at Veronda with a smile. "Can I please get another one?"

Veronda poked her lips out for him to kiss her."Mmmmm-mah," she uttered, as their lips touched again.

"Now c'mon, let's go inside," said Derrick.

The three of them headed inside. Once inside, Veronda told Mike-Mike to have a seat. Mike-Mike took a seat on the sofa. As he did so, he witnessed Derrick whispering something in Veronda's ear. He didn't know what Derrick was saying to her. But Mike-Mike noticed she was smiling at him the whole time Derrick was whispering in her ear.

"Have you ever had sex, Mike-Mike?" Veronda asked, as she came and sat next to him on the sofa.

Mike-Mike shook his head. "Nope, I've never had sex. My mother told me that I should wait until I get married."

Veronda looked back at Derrick.

"That's only if it's not your birthday. Besides, Momma ain't here," said Derrick, rolling up a blunt. "Now take your pants down. Veronda has a surprise for you."

Mike-Mike did as his brother said. He pulled both his pants and underwear down and sat back down on the sofa. "Relax, okay, Mike-Mike?" Veronda said reassuringly.

Mike-Mike lay back on the couch. Veronda bent over with one knee on the couch, massaged his dick until it was solid hard, then placed her mouth over it and licked around the head of it like it was her favorite flavored lollipop. Mike-Mike closed his eyes and inhaled air through his teeth. Derrick puffed on his blunt and watched the birthday boy enjoy himself. "How does it feel, li'l bruh? Do you like it?" he asked, releasing weed smoke from his lungs.

"It feels gooooood. Ooooo."

Veronda stopped only to stop herself from laughing hard. She then said, "Hush, Derrick, and let your little brother allow me to light the fire on his candle."

"You got that, boo-boo."

Veronda again placed her whole mouth on and over Mike-Mike's hard dick. She tightened her jaws and started moving her tongue around and around on his dick.

"Derrick, b . . . bruh, this isss a . . . mazing."

Derrick took a hard drag from his blunt, then put it in an ashtray. "I know it feels amazing; I'm really getting jealous," he said as he eased up behind Veronda. He placed his hand underneath her skirt, slid her panties to the side, and started rubbing up, down, and around her clit and fingering her spot. Derrick's finger felt so wonderful inside her tight, wet hole that giving Mike-Mike head became difficult. "Stay focused, baby. Stay focused," Derrick commanded. Mike-Mike had a look on his face like he didn't know whether to pay attention to what his brother was doing behind Veronda, or pay attention to Veronda's mouth moving up and down on his dick. He looked like he was in heaven with a big smile pasted on his lips.

Instead, he laid his head back, closed his eyes, and enjoyed the ride. Veronda looked up at Mike-Mike as she pulled her skirt up to her back. Derrick knew emphatically that this was an indication for him to slide every bit of his eight-and-a-half inch, thick, hard dick inside her. He did so without delay, holding her panties to the side in the process. He started deep dickin' her slowly.

"Mmmmm," she moaned. Derrick stroked her pussy so good she nearly bit down on Mike-Mike.

How in the hell could Fat Jerome have wanted to fuck my bitch up her asshole when her pussy hole is so muthafuckin' on fire? This bitch of mines got the best snapper in Charlotte.

"Derrrrrick, bruh, what is this I'm feeeeeling? It tickles."

"You're feeling what I'm feeling, li'l bruh. It's called 'nuttin'.' It's one of the greatest feelings you'll ever feel in your life. Enjoy it; it'll only last a few seconds."

"Derrick, you crazy, boy." Veronda laughed. "Now I gotta take another bath."

"Clean my little brother up, too, boo-boo."

"I got him," she replied. "Hold on. Stay there a minute, Mike-Mike, I'll be right back." Veronda returned with some baby wipes. She cleaned Mike-Mike up and kissed him on the cheek. "Once again, happy birthday!"

Mike-Mike just stood there. He was dazed from the head she had just given him. Never had he experienced an orgasm. Veronda had delivered him his first.

"What you say to that, Mike-Mike?" asked Derrick.

"I . . . I don't know."

"You say, 'Miss Veronda, that felt good. Can you do it to me again before I leave to go home?'"

"Miss Veronda, that felt good. Can you—"

Veronda cut him off with a laugh. "Maybe next year on your birthday."

"Tell her thank you, anyway," said Derrick.

"Thank you, Ver . . . Veronda."

Veronda blew him a kiss. "You're welcome, handsome."

Derrick then looked at Mike-Mike. "Wait on me in the car. I'll be there in a second."

Mike-Mike exited. When he did, Derrick told Veronda to get his coke out the stash. As she followed up on his request, he went into the bathroom to wash his dick. There was no way he was gonna be moving around in the Queen City smelling like pussy.

He walked into Veronda's bedroom. "Here you go," stated Veronda, handing him his bag full of coke.

As she stood before him, he cupped her ass cheek, and kissed her on her top lip then her bottom. "Thank you for fuckin' rockin' my li'l brother's world. Shit, I know he'll never forget you or that good-ass head you delivered."

Veronda smiled shyly. "You crazy, Derrick boy, I'm serious. You crazy."

"Here, take this and go to the mall," he said, pulling a wad of cash from one of his front pockets. He peeled off $1,200.

"Thank you, boo-boo. Now, when am I gonna see you again?" Veronda asked.

"Later."

"What's later, Derrick?"

"I can't give you a definite, baby. I'll just pop up when I pop up."

"Why can't you just give me a definite? You always say that shit."

"'Cause the streets don't allow you to give definites. I'm caught up in this world of sin, motivated by dividends. Anything could fuckin' happen and you know that. But if in the process of me doing wrong out here in these streets, I happen to make it another minute, hour, or day, I count it a blessing from the Big Man upstairs. You do know He looks out for thugs too, right?"

"Derrick, God looks out for us all. For how long is the question."

"Well, hopefully, forever. Now, I'll be back later, baby. Don't worry," Derrick said between kisses and squeezing her booty. Veronda's booty felt like cotton in his hands it was so soft. Had it not been for him having to get Mike-Mike back home, and him needing to get rid of the coke, he would have put that dick back up in her again. Instead, he tucked his bag of coke in his pants, checked for his gun at his waist, and bounced.

4

Don't Tell Momma

"Derrick, bruh, this has been the best birthday of my life. Man, I'm for real," exclaimed Mike-Mike. He was so excited about getting his dick sucked.

Derrick smiled. "You really enjoyed yourself, huh?"

"Did I? Man, bruh, your girlfriend is amazing. I see why you in love with her."

"Well, I'm glad you're happy about that. It makes me feel good when I see you happy. When I was your age, very few things made me happy. But I didn't go around trippin' and whatnot about it. I did what Momma wanted me to do, which was concentrate hard on my schoolwork. I'm out of school now. I walked across that stage with honor. Seeing the smile on Momma's face when I did so was more fulfilling to me than actually receiving my diploma. She always stayed on me about finishing school, like I stay on you, Mike-Mike. She wanted me to do other things like join the military, but sometimes things don't always go as we want them to. You feel me, Mike-Mike?"

"I think so."

"But you . . . you gotta finish school. A young black man ain't got no place in this society without a good education. Even if you've got a good education, the cards are still somewhat stacked against you because of your skin color."

"My skin color? What you mean by that, bruh?"

"What I mean is there are some people who think they are better than you because they're white. See Mike-Mike, many years ago our forefathers were kidnapped by white thugs and brought over here to America from our homeland, Africa."

"Trust me, I understand all of that and I've heard it before."

"Maybe you have, but hear me out, okay? Our forefathers were brought here to be made slaves. Under the white thug slave owners' system, our forefathers were stripped of a lot of things."

"Yeah, I get it, but when you say stripped, what are you referring to, bruh?"

"They were stripped of things like the knowledge of God, their identity, their culture, and just their basic way of life."

"Why would a person do this to another person? Isn't such treatment of human beings considered a crime?"

"That type of treatment of people today is a crime, because slavery has been abolished. You do know who abolished slavery, don't you?"

"Of course. Abraham Lincoln, in what, 1863, with the signing of the Emancipation Proclamation?"

"Right. But the slaves weren't set free until 1865. To answer your question as to why would a person do this to another person? Well, li'l bruh, I don't have all the answers, but I can say this: some people are just straight-up evil. They judge you by the color of your skin, rather than by the content of your character. This is why you, a young black man, gotta work extra hard in the area of getting your education. Not just that, but those manners that Momma be teaching you to use, well, those manners are what's gonna really open up doors for you. Momma taught me when I was your age to respect others and be courteous and all that. But being out here hustling in the streets, one learns to only respect those who have earned it. You, however, don't belong in the streets and as long as I'm alive you're not gonna end up in the streets."

Derrick pulled up to their apartment. "Now promise me one thing, Mike-Mike."

"What's that, bruh?"

"Promise me that you'll never tell Momma what Veronda did to you. You know she'll kill me if she found out I let you get your little wee-wee wet."

"I promise, bruh, I won't ever say anything about what happened today."

"If you do, I'm not ever gonna do anything special for you again, and I'm serious, Mike."

"Bruh, trust me on this one, I'll never go running my mouth. You can bank on that."

"A'ight, good. I'll see you later when I come back home." Derrick dropped Mike-Mike off and went to make some coke sales.

5

Yeah, I Know The Nigga

"I don't give a damn about that young nigga! As far as I'm concerned, he can kiss my red ass!" spat Monalisa to Tye-Tye. Monalisa was a Spanish chick who lived not too many blocks away from Derrick. "The nigga real disrespectful and shit, anyways!"

Tye-Tye had picked Monalisa up on the west side after inquiring about Derrick. "Is that a fact?" replied Tye-Tye, allowing the chick a seat inside his car.

"You damn right. Let me tell you what the nigga did. He rode past my father's house Sunday morning, blasting the fuck out of his music. My father was sitting on his porch as he did every morning, just minding his own business and being peaceful. The nigga slowed his car down right in front of our house. His music was so loud I could hear our windows in the house rattling. I looked out my window to see who it was and discovered that it was Derrick. I knew him because the nigga done sold me coke before. But anyway, I heard my father yell to him something like, 'Turn that music down.' The nigga said something to my father, and then gave my father his middle finger. My dad is seventy-one years old. He didn't deserve that."

"I can feel you on that," Tye-Tye responded.

"So yeah, I know the nigga." Her saying that was all Tye-Tye was interested in hearing. He had already killed Rasco, and wasn't gonna sleep until he got to Derrick.

"Well, check this out. Will a few of these make you tell me where I might be able to find him?"

Monalisa stared down at the small bags of crack-cocaine that Tye-Tye made visible in the palm of his hand. Her eyes got big and she started scratching her leg. "*Por esa cocaina,* I'll tell you exactly where you can find him."

"'Preciate it," Tye-Tye replied, as they rode to the location that Monalisa would point out.

It was approaching two o'clock in the morning when Derrick made it his business to head home. He figured he'd been out long enough. After he had gone and made some coke sales, he headed back to Veronda's place, put that thug dick on her, then had to be on his way.

"Baby, you leaving?" asked Veronda.

"Sweetheart, I have to. It's very late, and my mother hates it with a passion when I don't come home. She'll be worried like a muthafucka."

"Well, call me," Veronda said.

"I will," Derrick assured her before grabbing his car keys and bouncing.

Derrick hit the highway, where to his surprise he received an unexpected call on his cell phone from a friend of his named Eric. Usually when Eric phoned him it was for coke, but not this time.

"Hello?" answered Derrick.

"Dee, this Eric, man. I got some news to drop on you, playa."

"Drop it, 'cause apparently it's important, you hittin' me on my phone this time of the morning."

"I think it is, dawg. At least that's what my vibe is telling me."

"Drop it, bruh."

"Some nigga came rolling through earlier, driving a snow white Lexus. The nigga was real dark skinned with a bald head and full beard. I couldn't see his eyes because he was wearing dark tinted shades. But he was asking a lot of cats around here if they knew you and shit. All the thoroughbreds didn't even entertain the nigga. We brushed the bitch off and kept it moving, so the nigga moved on. However, that crackhead-ass Spanish bitch, Monalisa, I saw her ass talking to the nigga. Man, she may have told that nigga something about you."

"Talking 'bout the Spanish bitch who always come up on the block, tryin' to get a nigga to fuck her for crack?" asked Derrick.

"Yeah. She ain't shit, Dee. The bitch'll do anything to get that monkey off her back."

"You right about that," replied Derrick.

"I just called you to let you know that, and for you to be careful. That dude didn't have a good vibe coming from him. Look like a killa to me. I swear he do. Just be careful, a'ight?"

"No doubt. Thanks for the heads-up."

"No problem."

Derrick folded his cell phone, killing his and EB's conversation. He knew that the guy who was apparently searching for him wasn't Fat Jerome. Fat Jerome was a high yella cat, with long dreadlocks like a Jamaican. But Derrick also knew that even though the description of the guy looking for him didn't fit that of Fat Jerome the guy had to be one of Fat Jerome's soldiers. Derrick didn't embrace fearful thoughts. Being in and of the streets, he had learned uncompromisingly to conquer all fears.

The streets taught him that fear was a wonderful servant, but a terrible master. And that no one embracing the coldhearted street way of life could do so trembling whenever the possibility of a confrontation presented itself. He retrieved his gun from underneath the driver's seat, placed it in his lap, and continued moving.

The streetlights in Derrick's hood were all out, causing the street to be pitch-black dark. The lights on the poles were all shot out on purpose by street hustlers to avoid being spotted easily by the cops while drug deals were being conducted.

At two-something in the morning, the hood looked empty to Derrick. Only one or two drug addicts could be spotted roaming around in search of their next hit of coke. About a hundred or so yards away from where Derrick lived though, something else caught his attention as he methodically drove through the hood. It was the snow white Lexus.

Derrick's heart began to pound hard in his chest at the sight of the car. He parked his, got out, and made his way toward the snow white Lexus. Derrick had his gun underneath his left armpit. And he was nothing but determined to confront whoever sat in the seat of the Lexus.

He approached it with his gun out, now pressed at his leg. The windows were so darkly tinted on the snow white Lexus that he couldn't at all see if anyone was sitting therein. He tapped on the window of the driver's side with his knuckles, but received no response. He then checked to see if perhaps the door was unlocked. It was. He opened it with his gun pointed forward. To his dismay, however, no one was sitting inside.

"You looking for me, young blood?" a male raspy voice said behind Derrick.

It was Tye-Tye. He had crept up on Derrick so quietly and unexpectedly that Derrick nearly pissed in his pants.

"Drop your gun easy now!" Tye-Tye demanded of Derrick, with his ten-inch switchblade at his neck. "Drop it now, or I'll cut your damn throat from one end to the next." Derrick reluctantly dropped his gun. "Good boy. Now hop in my car; we're going for a li'l ride."

"He ain't going nowhere, nigga! Now drop that knife, or I swear I'll blow your brains all over your pretty white Lexus. Drop it, I said, and turn him loose!"

Tye-Tye hesitated a second or two. He couldn't believe someone had outsmarted him by catching him from the blind side.

"Nigga, I said drop the motherfuckin' knife!"

Tye-Tye dropped the knife and released Derrick. Derrick immediately retrieved his gun from the ground and saw that the man who had saved his throat from being slashed was Eric B.

"I saw this nigga's car parked over this way after I called you, Derrick, and figured his ass was up to something. Now, lie flat on ya stomach, bitch, and place your hands behind your back," Eric B. shouted, with his gun positioned at the back of Tye-Tye's head. Tye-Tye did as Eric B. ordered. "Find something to tie this bitch up with, Derrick."

Derrick looked inside Tye-Tye's Lexus's glove compartment. There he discovered some duct tape. He took the duct tape and wrapped it tightly around Tye-Tye's wrist.

"I'ma place him in the back seat with me while you drive, Eric B. A'ight?" said Derrick.

"A'ight, my nigga. Where to?"

"Just hit the nearest highway and ride," replied Derrick.

Eric B. took Tye-Tye's car keys from his left front pocket, waited until Tye-Tye and Derrick were inside the car, then drove off.

6

Your Boss Man Crossed Me

"I'ma be straightforward with you, my nigga. I know Fat Jerome sent you. And, I know you probably was gonna kill me, or hurt me up real bad because of the money that I was supposed to give Fat Jerome. But, listen, your fucking fat boss man crossed me."

"Crossed you?" Tye-Tye repeated. "Fat Jerome ain't got no reason to cross anybody."

"Shut the fuck up and listen!" Derrick seriously suggested. Tye-Tye bit down on his bottom lip and dropped his head.

"Your boss man crossed me when he crossed my woman. You know Veronda very well. She's my girl. Fat Jerome knew that when he got her drunk at a party he threw about a month ago. While Veronda was pissy drunk, you know what that fat, greedy, cocaine-dealing motherfucka did? He fuckin' took her in a room and sodomized her."

"What you mean, he 'sodomized' her?" Tye-Tye shot back.

"I mean, he had anal sex with her. And, let me add, without her fuckin' permission! She didn't want to tell me, but after refusing to allow me to touch her, she decided to tell me why. When she told me what your fat-ass boss did, my first reaction was to call him over to the place where he and I always meet and blow his fuckin' brains out. But Veronda told me to let it go! I couldn't let that shit go, though. I had to somehow fuck him just as he had fucked my girl. So, I refused to pay him. Now, here you come with your knife at my throat. Had it not been for my friend, you probably would have led me off somewhere and sliced it."

"It is what it is, dawg. I'm a killa!" replied Tye-Tye, lifting his head and looking forward, extremely disappointed with his present situation, for he knew not the outcome.

"So you're a killa for that fat bitch-ass perverted nigga, Jerome, huh?" Derrick spat.

"I do what I do, simple as that. What you gon' do? Shoot me? If I die, I die."

Derrick discerned that Tye-Tye was a cold-hearted vicious muthafucka. He didn't focus much attention on that, though. He knew that Tye-Tye was from the streets, and the streets breed guys like Tye-Tye every second. Derrick also knew that very few slip from these types of niggas' death grips.

"I do what I do, young blood. You know how it fuckin' is out here in this jungle where fuckin' only the strong move on and the weak get stepped on. It's dammit live or die. And, if you're working for someone who is taking real good care of you, the code is to be as loyal as possible. Fat Jerome is my main man. He's a good dude, loyal to those who are loyal to him. The nigga can have any bitch in this city. Some of them will fuck him for free! Others have hidden agendas. That's why it's hard for me to believe that he would stoop so low as to fuck Veronda in her ass without her wanting him to. That's if what you're telling me is true. There's a lot of lying-ass niggas out here," Tye-Tye spat.

"Dawg, I don't have no fuckin' reason to lie to you. Neither did Veronda have any reason to lie to me. She's my girl and I fuckin' believe her!"

"Veronda is a sweet girl. I've been knowing her for a while. She's done a lot of favors for our crew. I just can't see Fat Jerome doing that to her. If he did, I wouldn't be able to see him as a thoroughbred gangsta anymore," Tye-Tye interrupted.

"Like I said, that's the reason I refused to give that nigga shit."

"Then that was your reason. Had it been my girl, somebody's throat would have gotten sliced."

"Maybe so. But I'm not a killa."

"Well, I am," Tye-Tye assured him, unashamed and unafraid.

"You are who you are. A zebra can't change its stripes, neither a leopard its spots."

"Well, I tell you what, young blood, and this is my word, which I am most loyal to. If you phone Veronda and let me speak with her and she tells me out of her own mouth that Fat Jerome fucked her as you said he did, then I'll personally do something about it."

"I'll do better than that. I'll call and have her meet us somewhere, so she can tell you," Derrick said.

"You're right. That would be even better," replied Tye-Tye.

"Okay, watch this." Derrick held with one hand his gun to Tye-Tye's head, while with his other hand he dialed Veronda's phone number.

"Hello," Veronda answered after letting the phone ring five times.

"Baby, what you doing?" said Derrick at hearing her voice.

"I was trying to fall asleep, but for some reason I can't," Veronda shot back.

"Look, I got . . . Wait a minute." Derrick looked over at Tye-Tye. "Yo, dawg, what they call you?"

"Tye-Tye. They call me Tye-Tye."

"I got Tye-Tye in the car with me—"

When Veronda heard that name she cut Derrick off. "Tye-Tye? Derrick, that's one of Fat Jerome's workers. That nigga is vicious! You betta—"

"I know and it's a long story, but I need for you to get up and meet me in the parking lot of Bruns Elementary school," Derrick shot back, cutting her off.

"Do you know what time it is? It's almost three o'clock in the morning, Derrick."

"Just do it, a'ight? This is important. Now, be there. I'll be waiting in an all-white Lexus."

Forty-five minutes later . . .

Veronda pulled into the parking lot of Bruns Elementary school. Not knowing what to expect, she was trembling on the inside. All she knew for sure was to look for a white Lexus. Finding it wasn't hard. She spotted it slap dead in the middle of the parking lot. She drove right up next to the driver's side and rolled her window down. Eric B. rolled the window down in the Lexus.

"Where's Derrick?" shouted Veronda.

"In the back," responded Eric B. "Come over here, Veronda."

Veronda killed her car engine, and then got out and headed toward the passenger side of the Lexus. When she entered the car and looked toward the back seat where Derrick was with his gun positioned at the side of Tye-Tye's head, she gasped in shock with her hands to her mouth. "Oh, my gosh, Derrick, what are you doing? I know you're not gonna kill him, are you?"

"Just tell him what Fat Jerome did to you," Derrick shot back.

All eyes were on Veronda at that moment. "I thought I told you to let that go, Derrick. Why we gotta go through this?" Veronda said, about to cry.

"Because that fat motherfucka sent this guy to kill me, that's why. Now, tell him the reason I held back on paying that fat bastard, Veronda."

Veronda hesitated. "Please, Derrick I don't wanna do this," she replied, nervously.

Tye-Tye stared hard at Veronda. Through the light in the car, he saw tears in her eyes, and that's when he interjected. "Did Fat Jerome sodomize you while you were drunk? Is that true? Yes or no."

Veronda looked over at Derrick.

"Tell him, Veronda. Shit, what's done is done."

Veronda then looked at Tye-Tye. She knew she was looking into the face of a guy who would kill on the drop of a dime for Fat Jerome. As if reading her very thoughts, Tye-Tye said, "Look, Veronda, nothing is gonna happen to you. Besides, your man here got my hands tied. He could blow my brains out if he chose. I just basically want to know the truth."

Veronda didn't want anyone getting hurt behind her. She hated guns and what guns could do, especially in the hands of someone unafraid to pull that trigger in aid of proving a point. Tears rolled down her face. Tears that Tye-Tye knew from just being a human being with street smarts indicated that this wasn't a playful matter with Veronda; his boss man must have violated her person.

"Tye-Tye, you know I wouldn't lie to you," Veronda said, wiping a tear from her cheek.

"I know you wouldn't, Veronda." Tye-Tye softened.

"Whatever Derrick told you is true. Fat Jerome did disrespect me in a manner that I definitely didn't appreciate."

"Well, say no more. If your man here will allow me then this is how I will handle the matter." Tye-Tye devised a plan, one which Derrick was more than eager to see come to fruition.

7

A Person Can Make His Mouth Say Anything

Mike-Mike awoke at nine o'clock sharp to the aroma of fried bacon. He followed the scent to the kitchen where he discovered his mother fixing the two of them breakfast. "Good morning, young fella. Finally decided to get up, huh?"

"I guess," Mike-Mike said through yawning while also rubbing his finger over his eye. "Where's Derrick?"

"Don't know. He didn't come in last night. Didn't call me yesterday either."

"I told him you said call you."

"Well, he didn't. More than likely he was high and forgot again."

Mike-Mike took a seat at the table. "Momma, why were you crying the other day when you were praying? Did my brother do something wrong?"

"Your brother just hardheaded and think he's got all the sense. Stuck on doing things his way."

"He told me the reason he do illegal stuff is so that he can help us get out the hood. Don't you want us out of here as soon as possible, Momma? I sure do. Every night somebody's shooting. And everywhere you turn, when walking down the streets, you see somebody on drugs. I be scared sometimes."

"Let me explain something to you, Mike-Mike," his mother said, placing a plate of hot grits, scrambled eggs, bacon, toast, and orange juice before him to eat and drink. "Your brother Derrick is my oldest son. You're my youngest. I love the both of y'all dearly, Mike-Mike. I would love for us to get out the hood as soon as possible, but some things take time. Besides, if we just be a little more patient, something special is gonna come through for us. However, your hardheaded brother can't see the forest for looking at the trees. He's a very bad example for you to follow. No real true big brother would ever allow his little brother to see him high off weed. Neither would a real true brother paint a picture that selling drugs is an option if you're doing so to get your mother out the hood."

"Derrick never painted that type of picture for me, Momma. He always tells me that selling drugs is wrong, and that he better never catch me dealing dope."

"I better never catch you selling them either. But that's what your brother's mouth says. A person can make his mouth say anything. But a tree is known by the fruit it bears. Derrick's actions speak louder than his words. He's a drug dealer. He says that he does so to help us get out the hood. But look at what he just did. He spent almost eighteen thousand dollars on a new car that he bought from some other drug dealer. He's got jewelry in his room worth thousands, as well as expensive clothes. When the neighbors see him they know automatically he's a drug dealer, because we live in the hood where the poor reside, yet he parades himself around like he's filthy rich. When an individual hustling in the streets is flashy and whatnot, either somebody's gon' rob him, or the police is gonna get hot on his trail, and that's when your brother will be calling us from jail. A place he definitely ain't trying to end up in."

"Why you think he wouldn't want to go to jail, Momma?" Mike-Mike asked with his mouth full and smiling.

"Because I've read enough prison stories to know that a lot of young boys who end up in jail or prison end up fighting for their manhood."

"By that you mean?"

"What I simply mean by that, Mike-Mike, is a young male may indeed enter prison as straight as they can be, but he may leave transformed into someone 'feminine.'"

"So you're saying he might get punked out?"

"That's how it is up in there."

"I don't think my brother would go for that. Nobody's punking Derrick out. Nobody!"

"Trust me, Mike-Mike, Derrick is not as strong and smart as you may think. Oh, I know your brother puts on this thuggish front. But, boy, hear me, there are some guys in prison doing time who are really hardcore and vicious. Some are there for being serial rapists. Others are there for being cold-blooded murderers. Many of them are never ever getting out. They would love to have some fresh meat to devour. That place is five times more violent than the hood could ever be. Because all you have there is a bunch of angry males who can't take their anger and frustrations out any other way except on each other. That's what makes a place like prison so very bad."

"Don't sound like a place I would want to be."

"Like I said, your brother wouldn't want to be there either. But if he doesn't come to his senses, straighten up, and fly right, that's exactly where he's headed or, worse, to an early grave. Now, as a mother, Mike-Mike, do you think for one moment that's what I want Derrick's future to look like?"

"No, ma'am. I know that's not what you want my brother's future to look like. But, Momma, my brother, like you said, is young. With him being young and all, can't you just somehow excuse his demeanor? I mean, like I heard you say once he's 'just a kid.'"

"Your brother is a kid, yes. But he is a kid who knows right from wrong. When you know better you ought to do better. In that regard, there is no excusing his demeanor."

"Not even a little bit, Momma?"

"Not even a little bit. Because your brother's so hardheaded and careless that if you give him an inch, he'll take a mile. Now eat your breakfast and tell me how you like your new computer I bought you for your birthday." Derrick's mother quickly changed the subject. Just thinking about Derrick's hard head gave her a headache. Talking about it was like asking for a migraine.

"Lord Jesus, get a hold of my son. Get a hold of him before some bullet does," she later prayed, down on her knees.

8

I Was Drunk

Inside of a liquor house on the north side of Charlotte, Fat Jerome and Tye-Tye sat at a table, drinking gin and orange juice. Tye-Tye proceeded to convince Fat Jerome to comply with the plan that he had devised. Among other things, Tye-Tye's plan included terminating Derrick's debt. Fat Jerome was hesitant. His pride would not allow him to let a nigga get away with owing him $25,000 for a kilo given on consignment.

"Business is fuckin' business, Tye. The nigga gotta go," Fat Jerome said on the matter.

Tye-Tye ignored his boss's order and madness and told him what Veronda had told him about being violated.

"Bullshit," Fat Jerome shot back in complete denial. "That bitch lying out of her ass, dawg."

Tye-Tye downed his glass of gin, shook his head in the negative, and got up from the table. He grabbed the bottle of gin from behind the bar, and then poured him and Fat Jerome another drink.

"You and I both been knowing Veronda for years, Fat Jerome. That girl has always been good to our crew. Never once has she crossed us in any way. Never once, man. She looked me squarely in my eyes without blinking and told me trembling that you violated her while she was pissy fuckin' drunk. Now, Fat Jerome, I've been loyal to you. I've never lied to you about anything. Nor have I ever betrayed you. You family to me. You're like my brother; the nigga Rasco, he's history. I sliced that nigga's throat so fast he didn't even see it coming. I did that because of my loyalty to you, because no street soldier should ever refuse an order from his general without a legitimate explanation."

"I know how you are, Tye-Tye. You're one of the most loyal soldiers out here," said Fat Jerome.

"Damn right I am. I only want to know the truth about this one, my nigga. Did you do that shit to her? Look me in my eyes and keep it real."

Fat Jerome knew that Tye-Tye was dead serious. Tye-Tye had never questioned him about anything before. There was no way he could lie to Tye-Tye with a straight face. Therefore, he stood up from the table and hit down on it hard with his fist. "Dawg, I was drunk, a'ight? I may have done the shit, but the bitch making a big deal out of nothing."

"She could have gone to the cops about that shit. She didn't, though. Which for real for real is a damn breath of fresh fuckin' air for you. Because going downtown for a charge like that could've really disrupted some things for you. And it's too damn much loot to get out here for the crew to lose you."

"Okay, okay. Well, it is what it is. Now what?"

"All I'm getting to is this: that young cat, Derrick, did what he did because he felt like you disrespected him by disrespecting his girl. Which, believe it or not, is understandable."

"Understandable?" Fat Jerome repeated. "Tye-Tye, what you mean it's understandable? The nigga owes us twenty-five thousand," Fat Jerome said, cutting Tye-Tye off.

"True, indeed. But which one of us wouldn't have done the same had someone violated a woman of ours? I mean, c'mon, man. The young brother felt offended."

"Yeah, but—"

"Fat Jerome, there are no buts about it in this matter. Right is right and wrong is wrong. We're gangsta-ass niggas, not rapists." When Tye-Tye made that last statement, an evil-ass look came over Fat Jerome's face. The type of evil look that Fat Jerome got when he was ready to order a hit on a nigga. Tye-Tye didn't give a fuck about his facial expression. To him, it was no more than the typical thug reaction.

"That's why I think we should let the young cat slide."

"Slide?" Fat Jerome repeated.

"Yeah. And dump thirty thousand dollars on Veronda for her troubles."

"Tye, are you fuckin' okay, man? Let young blood slide and drop thirty stacks on that stinking-ass bitch, Veronda? C'mon, man. That's a bit steep, don't you think?"

"Fuck naw, man. For real for real, peep this, man. I was close as a muthafucka to killing young blood last night. I crept up on his ass real good. You already know how I do it. I had my knife at the young nigga's throat and everything. But out of nowhere one of his partners crept my ass from the blind side, with a gun aimed straight at the back of my head. The nigga was gonna kill me. So, I honestly couldn't do anything but surrender. It took a lot for me to surrender to two young cats, who under any other circumstances I would have taken out with no problem.

"Making a long story short, young blood and 'em could have killed me and dumped my body in an undisclosed location. But the two niggas spared me. That's the real reason I would like for you to terminate the nigga's debt. The issue with Veronda, man, she was fuckin' crying. The chick really felt violated."

"Man, fuck her! But for you, Tye-Tye, I'ma comply with your suggestion, 'cause, dawg, you my nigga. I could never refuse you. But when you drop that money off on that stinkin'-ass bitch, Veronda, you make sure you tell that bitch I betta never ever see her in this city again. No bullshit! The same goes for—"

"Man, just let young blood go," Tye said, cutting him off. "Just let him go."

"Tye, man, the nigga just betta never show his head over on the north side. And I'm through with that."

In conjunction with keepin' his word, Tye-Tye sought not to hurt or harm Derrick in any way, in spite of how his boss, Fat Jerome, felt about the situation overall. After Tye-Tye delivered the $30,000 to Veronda and told Derrick what was up along with her, the two of them never saw Tye-Tye again.

A month later, Veronda decided to pack her shit and move to the ATL. She did so, worrying that Fat Jerome would indeed kill her if she remained in the city he hustled out of. Derrick in no way wanted her to leave. It pained his heart that she would consider the action, or even the thought. Next to his mother, Veronda was his number one sweetheart.

"Please, boo-boo, don't go," he pleaded. "My mom, little brother, and I will be in our own place soon. You can stay with us. I promise I'll protect you from any assault that fat nigga may try to bring your way. Baby girl, that's my word. What you think I got this big-ass gun for? You think I won't use the muthafucka when it comes down to protecting you? I love you."

Veronda caressed his cheek, as he assured her of his protective love. "Baby, I know you love me. And I know you knee deep in the game with a lot of muscle and a lot of heart. But that nigga, Fat Jerome, will stop at nothing to see me dead. I know that nigga. The nigga got other killas on his team, trust me. Tye-Tye is not the only one. Tye-Tye is just like maybe his top lieutenant. The nigga got a capo by the name of Osama. They call him O for short. Tye and 'em other niggas ain't as cold as this nigga," Veronda assured him.

"How you know this nigga?" Derrick asked.

"Fat Jerome talks a lot when he drinks. Plus, as I was riding with him one night to drop off some heroin, he took me to meet Osama. Fat Jerome told me out of his own fuckin' mouth that the nigga specializes in getting rid of mutha-fuckas for him. He said the nigga had more bodies than a graveyard. Real talk, Derrick."

"So, why are you just telling me about this nigga, Veronda?"

Veronda sighed. "Honestly, Derrick, I forgot all about the nigga. See, he ain't like some of Fat Jerome's other hit men. He doesn't hang out. He keeps a very low profile. In fact, the nigga been in hiding for a while."

"In hiding?" said Derrick, puzzled. "In hiding for what?"

"According to Fat Jerome, and like I said he talks a lot when he drinks, the nigga Osama set a dude's home on fire one night while the dude's wife and kid was inside. They all burned to death. The dude was allegedly a big-time heroin dealer from Africa. I think he was a Nigerian. He was supposed to have been the guy who put Fat Jerome on his feet."

"Yeah, but why would Fat Jerome allow that to be done to someone who was good to him?" asked Derrick.

"They had some type of money dispute. Fat Jerome owed the nigga a lot of money. Money that Fat Jerome had fucked up in Vegas, gambling."

"Oh, I see," Derrick replied. "That's still fucked up, though."

"Yeah. Since he couldn't pay up, he had the nigga and his family killed. Then he raided the nigga's stash spot."

"Daaamn," Derrick shot back, shaking his head in the negative.

"The nigga's dirty as fuck, yo. That's why I can't take any chances staying here in Charlotte, Derrick. I just can't. Especially knowing that the nigga Osama never misses a target," Veronda concluded.

Derrick secretly cried within for many days after Veronda's departure. If her leaving was a .357 Magnum, his heart would have been blown away, and he literally would have been in a casket six feet deep underground. That's how devastating her absence was to him. He didn't have anyone to hug, kiss, and fuck from damn near any position like he and Veronda used to do. True enough, he was a drug dealer with a lot of cash, which caused other chicks to run with Marion Jones' speed to suck his dick and fuck him. But none of them chicks, who really only wanted to be with him because of his money, looks, and nice-ass car could touch him with the intimacy that Veronda delivered.

Therefore, to cloud the reality of the pain that her absence brought his way, he started smoking blunts without restraint. He was sky high all day, all night, and in between. Until one evening, about four months after Veronda had made the ATL her new home, a cop pulled his ass over for a busted taillight. He casually walked up to Derrick's car then bent down to observe the inside.

"Sir, I need to see your driver's license and registration," the officer said in a snobby tone.

Derrick quickly got defensive. "For what? Why do you need to see my license and registration?"

"Because I asked for it, that's why. Now, do you have a license or not?"

Derrick released a deep sigh, before reaching for his wallet in his back pocket. That's when he looked down and saw the butt of his .44 Desert Eagle sticking out from underneath the seat. He was so fuckin' high, he forgot it was there. He hoped the cop hadn't seen it, but unfortunately for Derrick, when he reached to give the cop his license, his eyes were locked on the gun.

"I need you to step out of the car, right now," the officer replied while touching his holster.

Derrick hesitated to make a move, but he soon realized that he didn't have many options before him. As soon as he got out of the car, the cop drew his weapon and informed Derrick that he was being arrested.

With disgust written all over his face, Derrick placed his hands behind his back. He knew that prison time awaited him, and several months later, he was sentenced to sixty months in a federal prison for the violation of carrying a concealed weapon without a permit.

Derrick didn't give a fuck. He felt that he had to arm himself while ripping and running the crucial coldhearted streets, hustling, especially after what Veronda revealed to him about the nigga Osama.

However, Derrick's mother was extremely hurt. When she heard the federal judge pronounce that sixty-month sentence to her son, she stood to voice her opinion.

"Sixty months! Oh, my Jesus! Fix this, please! This is so unfair. Derrick was set up and that gun didn't belong to him! I . . . I can't believe how fucked up this system is!"

Several officers approached Derrick's mother, trying to calm her down. She continued to voice her opinion loudly, and when one of the officers attempted to escort her out of the courtroom, she snatched away from him and shoved him backward.

"Don't you dare put your filthy, grimy hands on me! My son is innocent! You hear me? He is innocent and y'all know it!"

The judge slammed down his gavel and asked the cops to clear the courtroom. Derrick shook his head while watching his mother's actions. Deep down, he knew he was guilty.

The second his mother exited the courtroom, she clenched her chest and fainted right smack dab in the middle of the floor. Several people came to her aid, and she had to be carried outside to get some fresh air. She just couldn't bear knowing that her son was about to be sent to prison, a place she had read so much about. And after that day, she prayed daily for God to watch over Derrick while he did his time.

Derrick's little brother wrote to him every week. Some of the letters Mike-Mike would give his mother to send Derrick left him in deep thought, as he stood in his jail cell reading them. Tears were at the rim of his eyes and his heart ached for his little brother. He didn't want Mike-Mike to experience any of this, and he truly felt as if he could have been a better role model. More than anything, he hoped that it wasn't too late for him or for Mike-Mike as well.

9

Dear Big Brother

Dear Big Brother, Derrick,

I am writing you while on my lunch break at school. I just couldn't stop thinking about you. You're on my mind constantly on a daily basis. I wish I could come to see you. But Momma told me that you didn't want her to bring me to visit you. She said that you didn't want me to see you caged in like an animal. However, I did get the picture you sent to me, as well as your letter. Thanks a lot, bruh. I put the picture on my wall in my room. I view it every day. I see that you're putting on some muscles. You must be lifting weights up in there. You look good, though.

You asked me to share with you how I am doing in school. Bruh, Momma didn't tell you? Man, I'm one of the top in my class in science and mathematics. I think I want to become a junior high school teacher and teach science one day.

Now I know you're probably saying, "Mike-Mike, I thought that you wanted to become a professional basketball player?" Well, bruh, to be honest with you, I haven't picked up a basketball since the day you left. When I used to dribble that ball in your presence, and show you the little moves and tricks that I could do with it, the look that I would see in your eyes was a look that would always read: My little brother gon' be somebody one day. Somebody like a little Michael Jordan. That look in your eyes always inspired me, Derrick. But now that you're far away, the inspiration is gone. Not just that. But your applause at my performance is gone, too, along with you. Everything I did when that basketball would be in my hands, I did to impress you, my big brother. Now I don't have you here to impress.

This hurts a lot, bruh, but I don't really want to bore you with how much it hurts. However, you have always told me to "Keep it real" with you at all times. So, really, *that's all I am attempting to do through this letter. It's extremely hard, though, bruh. It's really hard. I mean, Derrick, you're my big brother. You are also the father I never had. You tell me a lot about our father, and how good of a guy he was, but the truth is I never knew him as you did 'cause I was an infant when he died. You have been my father; when I needed things that Mom couldn't afford to buy me, you bought them. When Momma couldn't give me an allowance because she had to pay bills and whatnot, you gave me one.*

And, yeah, I know that you only were able to do those things through hustling in the streets. That's why, man, I could never look down on you. I knew that some of the things you were doing were wrong, because Momma would always tell me. She hated the example you set for me to follow. But hey, you are who you are, and I love you, always and forever.

Anyway, bruh, when I look back I can say for sure that none of the material things you gave to me could ever equate to having your actual presence here with me right now. Man, Derrick, I would do anything to have you home. I swear. Because your presence means the world to me. Nothing material could amount to it. I know that Momma feels the same way. Man, she hasn't stopped crying since you left. She thinks that someone will end up hurting you up in there. Sometimes I feel the same way too. But I know deep down inside that my big brother can handle himself.

Like I was saying though, bruh, nothing beats having you here with us. So I hope that while you are there you will take advantage of every opportunity available to better yourself. Momma said that you told her that the place where you're at offers a lot of vocational training courses. Please, Derrick, bruh, do what you gotta do, so that you can come home to Momma and me and never leave us again. I simply can't take you being away from us a second time. I can hardly take this one. I just miss you a lot, bruh. Sometimes the brother of one of my friends here at school comes to pick him up. When I see that, I immediately think of you and wish that you were home to pick me up from school so that we could ride around and go to a McDonald's or something like that.

Bruh, please hurry home. I love you,
Your baby brother

P.S. I know Momma told you already,
but we finally got our own home. The
elderly lady Momma been working for all
these years blessed her with one. The lady
owns a lot of them. Man, Derrick, I love
it, too. No drug dealers, no drug fiends,
none of those negative things in our new
neighborhood. Man, it's beautiful. So like
I said, do the right thing and come home.

"The intelligence of a man is not defined by what he read in a book, but rather in his ability to exercise common sense when the time and moment call for nothing less."
—K. Tomblin

10

Dear Mike-Mike

Dear Mike-Mike,

Li'l bruh, this place is most vicious. I thought living in the ghetto was a headache and a discouragement, but prison is all of the above and more. I had absolutely no idea just how much being in this place would help change the way I see myself doing things in the future. I cannot go where I wanna go, do what I wanna do, say what I wanna say in this place being that it's prison and the authorities run it with an iron fist. I mean, bruh, they tell you what to do, how to do it, and when to do it. If you buck and rebel they send you straight to solitary confinement. In solitary confinement you can't use the telephone. Neither can you come out of your room, except for one hour to get some recreation. Inside your room in solitary confinement there's a small shower stall, a sink, and a toilet. There is also a desk to write on. How do I know this? Well, I told Momma not to tell you. I wasn't gonna tell you either, because I didn't want you to worry about me. But I have been in solitary confinement for the last month and a half. I got into a fight with a guy for trying to break into my locker and steal my radio. I caught the guy right in the act.

When I walked in on him his eyes got big as the eyes of an owl. I confronted him with a punch straight to his jaw. Because in here, Mike-Mike, when someone tries to take something from you it's a sign that they see you as weak. Since I had just got to this institution I guess the guy thought I was green as spring grass, but a homie of mine had already put me up on the game. He told me that I was gonna be tried because I was new.

Excuse my street language, bruh, but I beat that dude's ass. The correctional officer had to get me up off his ass, no bull-shit. They gave me ninety days in solitary confinement for my actions despite me telling them that the reason I was fighting was because I caught this guy trying to steal my radio from my locker. In here they really enforce you abiding by the rules. You don't abide by the rules, you get your ass spanked by the administration.

Before they put me in solitary confinement, guess what they did? They put me in a cell (room) with a guy who had been severely abused. He got transferred, but he certainly left scarred. He was a young white guy, twenty-two years old to be exact.

Guess what he told me happened to him, Mike-Mike? He told me that he was approached by these two big-ass guys. They both were weightlifters and serving a lot of prison time.

He said they caught him coming out the shower with nothing on but his boxer underwear and shower shoes. They waited 'til he entered his room and went inside behind him. Without any warning, one grabbed him while the other pulled his boxer underwear down and completely off. He said the both of them were so strong that he was unable to fight them. One of them pulled out a shank (homemade prison knife) and put it to his throat and told him that if he hollered for the correctional officer to help him, he would never have to worry about ever seeing the free world again because he would be a dead man. "Please, just tell me what do y'all want with me? Is it money? I can get you money," he said to them. They didn't want money. One wanted oral sex. The other anal. And like many strong predators in here, they got what they wanted from their weak prey. Both of these guys took advantage of this young white guy. He later initiated going into PC (Protective Custody) after revealing to the administration what had happened to him.

He told me that he had to tell them what had happened to him, because he needed medical attention. The two guys who violated him are now somewhere in solitary confinement and facing rape charges. But that's the way it is in here, Mike-Mike. That's why I sent you those pictures of me with my shirt off, to show you that I have been lifting weights and working out hard. A person can't appear weak at all in here. He'll get his ass beat, or raped. These guys in here are so aggressive they'll bump into *you on purpose just to check your temperature and see where you stand. Well, they know where I damn stand now. Me fighting has cost me ninety days in solitary confinement where I am writing you from, but hey, what was I to do? Let a nigga take what belongs to me?*

Nonetheless, little brother, besides all of that drama, I want you to know that your most recent letter to me left me in tears. Not because I'm someone soft, but because I had absolutely no idea as to how my thuggish behavior, which landed me here, would affect you and Mom. I miss you and her like crazy. Every day, Mike-Mike, the two of you are on my mind. And I want to apologize for leaving you. It was never my intention to hurt you, or Mom. Man, I just wanted to be in a position to generate monies to help Mom get our asses out the hood. But I failed and landed myself a first-class ticket in prison. Momma warned me, but when you're caught up, you're caught up. It's hard to hear good, sound advice when your thuggish ways have deafened your ears and blinded your eyes.

Being a thug in the streets as I had become, Mike-Mike, I knew I wasn't the best example for you to follow. No thug is, and I would be the first to admit this. Because selling drugs, regardless of the amount of money an individual is capable of making from it, just isn't the way to go. Neither is carrying guns and getting high as I was doing off of weed constantly. Man, I felt like I had to have that blunt every day, because I felt I needed it to cloud the pain of our father leaving at such a young age. Since I've been incarcerated though, without that weed to smoke on, I see that I really didn't need it. I doubt that I'll ever smoke any again.

Also, little brother, one day I will share with you how I damn near lost my life while thuggin' in the streets. Yeah, I came close to death, which is another thing I have thought heavily on. I thought about how if I would have gotten killed, you would have mourned your eyes out night and day. And Momma probably would have had a nervous breakdown.

Man, she loves the two of us so much, Mike-Mike. It brings tears to my eyes even now to think of the sacrifices our mother has made on our behalf. That's why when she came to visit me, I made it my business to let her know that it's certainly not her fault that I ended up in prison. The blame is on me. I point the finger toward myself for wanting to do things my way. And, my way, little brother, was the thug way, as I shared with you earlier. Momma taught me right from wrong. She taught me the difference between the color black and the color white. So, I knew better. And it pains my heart at this moment that I hurt her with my hardheadedness, and now my absence from the two of you.

As a result, I am gonna do everything in my power to never ever sell coke again, or hang out in the streets all times of the night, making Momma worry about whether or not I'm gonna walk through her front door. It's just not worth being in here in an abnormal environment, away from you and Momma. So when I get out of solitary confinement, trust me, and you know I have never lied to you, Mike-Mike, I'm going to read more and take as many classes as I can. I was already taking a vocational trade in welding prior to me getting into a fight.

Above all though, I'm gonna avoid being around guys in here who are not trying to change. I know that change won't come easy for me since thuggin' is in my blood. But nothing worth having comes easy. It *takes a lot of work, which I am willing to put in because I need to. I never want to leave you and Mom again, Mike-Mike. So, expect me to give change my best shot. In the meantime, little brother, I want you to stay focused on your schoolwork. Remember what I always shared with you: a black man in America is nothing without a proper education. Neither is a white man. So, get your education. Also remember this: drug dealers run corners and little after-hours spots; but intelligent, educated brothers run companies, corporations, cities, and countries.*

What I'm saying is, it doesn't take anything to become a drug dealer, or a thug. An idiot can do that. But an idiot can't run a company, or a corporation. This is what I have come to understand, little brother. That's why, if I can help it, I will never be that desperate young guy who went about trying to accomplish the goal of getting his mother and little brother out the hood the thug way, which is the wrong way, again.

I love you, little brother. See you when I get home.

Derrick

11

Capone And Night-Night

Back in the Queen City of Charlotte, far from where Derrick was serving prison time in South Carolina, trouble was in the air. Trouble that not even a strong wind from Mother Nature could blow away.

"I gotta get that nigga for what he did to my goddamn brother. Straight up! I know it was him," said Capone, Rasco's older brother, who was a notorious robber of drug dealers. He had just been released from prison and was out to execute thug justice on the nigga who was responsible for slicing his brother's throat. When he heard about what had happened to his brother while he was in the joint, he put his brother Rasco's picture on top of his locker and made a vow that he would do everything in his power to find the nigga who dared to do this to his blood.

He was a month fresh out of prison, and the matter was still fresh on his mind. "I know it was him, because word on the streets is that nigga Tye-Tye the only gangsta out here who cut nigga's throats as his method of killing. That's the nigga's signature."

"Really?" a nonchalant feminine voice said.

"Damn right, baby girl. And I got to see that nigga for what he did."

"I'm with you, baby. You know that. Just let me know the type of plate you wanna serve the nigga on once we catch up to him," she hissed. Her name was Shelia Brookly, but Capone referred to her as Night-Night. She was his ace, thorough and down for whatever. Capone nicknamed her Night-Night because whenever she went to see a nigga on Capone's behalf, it equated to "lights out, party over!"

"I wanna serve the nigga on a hard plate. Nothing soft, baby girl, about this mission," Capone said.

"Good. Do you know where we can find him?" Night-Night replied.

"Yeah. I know exactly where the nigga lives."

"That's even better," Night-Night said. "That's even fuckin' better."

Night-Night wasn't a street or hood chick at all until she met Capone, whose real name was Calvin. His thug ways viciously rubbed off on her. She was from a two-parent home. Her mother and father both loved her dearly and ensured that Night-Night lacked nothing growing up. She was her mother and father's only child, and they had great hopes that she would take advantage of educating herself, and making something meaningful out of her life. Thing was, she was attracted to thug guys. She didn't know why, but she loved their street swagger and ruffneck demeanor. She didn't like soft, nerdy, too-polite guys, because being feisty, headstrong, and aggressive, she could run over them.

Capone was the type of cat who fit the bill for her. He was tall, light, and handsome. He wore his baseball caps turned backward, he wore his shirts big to better hide his gun, and wore his pants saggin' like the drunks on the corner. He never tied his Timb boots. He wore the laces loose, the thug way.

It took Capone a little time to get Night-Night, because she didn't want a drug dealer. But Capone pursued her relentlessly. His thug charm eventually drew her into his world. And his street swagger and "rough around the edges" attitude kept her in check while in his life.

Once she became his girl, though, he began transforming her from good girl to thug girl. He taught Night-Night how to aim a gun straight at a target and shoot with accuracy. He taught her how to fight with her fists like a guy and not swing wildly with her hands. Capone even taught his thug queen to sell coke.

"Baby girl," he said to her once, "crack-cocaine can put a helluva lot of paper in our pockets. So, if you're gonna be my sidekick, you gotta do as I do and sell this shit." To please him, she did so. Before she knew it, selling drugs was like second nature to her.

However, when a guy was spotted once by Capone looking at Night-Night and trying to holler at her in spite of Capone being not too many steps behind her as they were coming out of a club, Capone pulled out his gun without warning, aimed it at the guy's head, and blew his brains into the atmosphere. That was the first time Night-Night ever saw someone die.

Later, Capone said to her, "Night-Night, out here in the streets you never let a nigga disrespect you or yours. You drop them like bad habits when they do that."

Everything Capone knew, he taught it to Night-Night. He didn't want them being unequally yoked together at all. He believed that only birds of a feather should flock together.

Now that Capone's brother was dead, the only person in his life he could trust was Night-Night, and she knew it. So when he looked to her to help him avenge his brother's death, it was lending her loyal hand to assist him that she could in no way refuse.

Capone and Night-Night stalked Tye-Tye's apartment for three days. They watched that nigga's movements compulsively, like they were the feds building a case against him. "Night-Night," Capone uttered, "I want you to get a lot of envelopes. Put them all in a big book bag and I want you to also have a lot of them in your hands. I'm gonna go to the Army/Navy clothing store and buy you an outfit."

"What do you have in mind, baby?"

"I want you to dress like a postal woman."

"A postal woman?" she repeated.

"Yeah, then give the nigga his mail, special delivery."

The sun was at its zenith and blazing hot, causing anyone under its mighty heat rays to perspire profusely. Night-Night was no exception. She walked toward Tye-Tye's apartment, carrying a big-ass book bag full of envelopes. She also had a nice amount in her hands just as Capone had directed her. Capone awaited her in a designated spot. He knew that if he stepped to Tye-Tye's door, it would be a dead giveaway. So this mission was one for Night-Night.

The both of them knew from stalking the nigga that he was home. His white Lexus was in the driveway. As Night-Night approached, her heart began to beat a little faster. She inhaled and exhaled deeply but slowly to calm her nerves. When she got up to Tye-Tye's front door, she was surprised to see him about to make an exit.

"You must be new," he said, spotting her at his door.

She wiped off the sweat that was forming on her forehead and running down her face. "I am new. In fact this is my first day on the job. Goshhh, it's hot out here. Could you get a girl a cold glass of water, please?"

Tye-Tye was so busy checking out how fine and thick Night-Night was that he didn't even hear her ask for cold water. He saw that Night-Night resembled rapper Lil' Kim. Her hair was nicely permed and hanging with streaks of blond in it. Her skin was light brown and she wore greenish contact lenses. She couldn't have been any taller than five foot three in Tye-Tye's sight and by the blouse she had on, her titties seemed to be too much for her bra as they poked outward graciously.

Night-Night's thighs and ass were hugging her pants so well that Tye-Tye would've gotten a hard-on had Night-Night not snapped him out of his trance-like lustful state by saying a second time, "You mind getting me a cold glass of water?"

"Oh, I'm sorry, cutie, my mind sometimes comes and goes whenever I'm in the presence of someone as beautiful as you. Anybody ever tell you that you look just like Lil' Kim?"

"I hear that all the time. Thanks for the compliment."

"You're welcome. By the way, I'm Tyrone. But everybody calls me Tye-Tye."

"Well, nice to meet you, Tyrone. I'm Shelia, your postal woman, but those close to me call me Night-Night."

"You can come in, Night-Night, or you can wait right here while I get your water."

Night-Night followed him inside. While he was walking toward his kitchen he heard her say, "Oh, and here's your mail." She passed an envelope to him. He turned his back to her to read the bold black letters written thereon that said, TODAY IS YOUR DAY, MUTHAFUCKA! When Tye-Tye turned around, the last thing he saw was fire spitting from the barrel of Night-Night's 9 mm.

12

Gangstas Come Gangstas Go

Outside in the parking lot of South Park Mall, Fat Jerome was carrying two brand spanking new boxes of peanut butter Timb with the bubblegum bottoms underneath his armpit, as he walked to his chromed-out sky blue Mercedes-Benz SL600 convertible.

In his other hand was his cell phone that was being held at his ear. "I simply can't believe this shit, Osama, man. I was just with Tye last night. How the fuck could he be dead?"

"Somebody caught him slippin'. You know things happen like that when you don't watch each and every move you make in the streets."

"The man's baby mother found him at his apartment with a hole in his head. In his apartment, Osama. Now who in the hell could have gotten that close to Tye? The man paid attention to every fuckin' thing. He rarely ever slipped."

"Don't matter now. He's history. We've gotta move on."

"Move on is right. But I gotta know who did this shit," Fat Jerome said, sitting inside his Benz with his door open and one leg outside.

"Oh, definitely."

"Tye was family, Osama. A big part."

"Could've been anybody though, Fat Jerome. Anybody. A lot of niggas out in the street feared him. He didn't play with these phony-ass niggas out here. He had enemies. All gangstas have enemies."

"All Tye's enemies are dead or somewhere hiding the fuck out."

"Apparently not."

Fat Jerome inhaled and exhaled hard through his nostrils. "What you suggest we do? Talk to me."

"We do what we must, Fat Jerome."

"Okay, I'm listening."

"We make inquiries. We find out what the streets are saying. If anything surfaces, we make who did it wish they hadn't."

"That's what I love about you, Osama, you keep everything simple."

"Well, I mean, why make things complex? Gangstas come and gangstas go. We don't like it when it hits home, but that's the reality of the way the ball rolls sometimes."

"You're right."

"We lick our wounds, but never tuck our tails."

"Oh, never that, my nigga. Never that," replied Fat Jerome.

Osama continued his discourse. "The life we live and seek to never renounce is a life of underworld activity. The ultimate fate is death, or a trip to the penitentiary. I am aware of this; you are aware of this; and, Tye, as a die-hard soldier, was aware of this. Tye earned his stripes the thug way. If a nigga out here doing illegal shit and can't learn to accept what comes with this life that we live, then such a nigga need to get his ass out of the streets 'cause out here there will be sad stories."

"Fo'sho, my nigga," Fat Jerome agreed.

"Now, with that said, what was that other business you wanted to discuss with me?"

"Veronda. Osama, you remember that chick, right?"

"The girl who used to strip and shit?"

"Yeah."

"What about her?"

"The bitch crossed me, man."

"What way?"

"Bitch told Tye I fucked her up her ass, absent her permission and shit."

"Did you?"

"I fucked the hell out of the bitch. But she makes it seem like I fuckin' raped her. I don't like that fuckin' shit."

"Did the bitch get the cops involved?"

"Nah. But Tye convinced me to give the chick a large amount of cash for her troubles."

"Her troubles? What fuckin troubles?" Osama shot back.

"Told you, man, the bitch made it seem like I fuckin' wanted her."

"Okay, so let me ask you this. Did Tye believe her?"

"Hell yeah. I told you he convinced me to drop some cash off on the bitch."

"How much did you drop on her, Fat Jerome?"

"Man, you don't wanna know."

"Then why would I ask? How much was it?"

"Thirty."

"Gs?"

"Thirty fuckin' Gs. Yep."

"See that's the only thing about Tye that I don't like."

"What's that?"

"He's soft for a woman. Tye was supposed to blow that bitch's heart out her chest for saying some shit like that."

"You feel me?" Fat Jerome asked.

"Do I? Damn right I feel you. Tye-Tye wasn't ever supposed to take that bitch's side."

"Now come to find out through this other stripper that Veronda been keeping in touch with, she's living in Atlanta."

"Is that right?" said Osama.

"Precisely."

"I suppose you want me to pay her a visit?"

"Precisely."

"How soon? And, what's the order?"

"I want you to see that bitch as soon as possible. The order is DNE: death, no exceptions!"

Putting that hit on Veronda in Osama's hands only meant that Fat Jerome now hated Veronda with a passion, and that her presence on earth had to have an expiration date, soon.

Osama got the message loud and clear. He checked the guns in his stash spot, got the one that he wanted, and made plans to kill Veronda.

13

I Did It For You, Baby

"You should have seen the look in his eyes right before I put him out of his misery, Capone."

"What they looked like, Night-Night?" asked Capone, as they chilled at the Adam's Mark hotel.

"Like they fuckin' saw a ghost!"

"Whuut?"

"No jokin', baby. I put two in his forehead and watched him drop to the floor."

"Thought I told you to only give him one to the head and let it be, Night-Night?"

"I know what you said. The nigga was big. I felt two was necessary. Plus, I didn't like how the nigga was eye-fuckin' me. He looked me up and down like I was a slave on an auction block."

"And you robbed the nigga?"

"No, not really. Just saw that his left pocket was poking out kinda nicely. Usually that means cha-ching."

"Eight grand ain't bad."

"He had that switchblade in his waistline. Decided to retrieve that, too. Probably what he used on your brother, and ain't no tellin' who the hell else."

"No probably in it. The nigga don't use guns. He never has. In fact, he told my brother once that guns make too much noise."

"Shit, that's what silencers are for," said Night-Night, as she watched Capone view the switchblade. It had about a three-inch pearl handle and about a seven-inch chrome sharpened blade. The blade was so razor sharp it could have cut a horse's throat, no problem.

"Fuckin' switchblade got my brother's blood all over it. I just know it. You gave that bitch-ass nigga what he fuckin' deserved, baby girl."

"I did it for you, baby," Night-Night responded. "Told you I'll do anything for you, Capone. You took a cocaine beef for me. How could I forget you for that? Huh?"

"It was just an ounce of powder, baby girl. I ain't sweatin' that shit."

"That's not the point. Point is, you sacrificed your life to go to prison for three and a half years for something that belonged to me."

"Doesn't make a difference, Night-Night."

"It does, Capone. You didn't know if I was gonna be true to you while you were serving your time."

"No, I didn't. I couldn't worry about that at the time though. All that mattered to me was not allowing my baby girl to go to prison. Luckily, you held me down while I was there, because I swear if you wouldn't have, I would have disowned you upon my release in a major way." When he was in prison, Night-Night visited every week and sent him money. He wanted for nothing.

"I'ma forever hold you down, baby boy. Forever," she said.

"Forev—" Before Capone could get "ever" out of his mouth, Night-Night's lips were on his.

"I deeply love you, Capone," she said between kisses. "You are a real nigga." Capone's realness alone made Night-Night's pussy wet.

"And you my bitch for life," Capone uttered, between kisses.

Night-Night stopped, and then looked him squarely in the eyes with her one finger over his lips. "Baby, don't refer to me as your bitch. A bitch is a female dog. And a female dog will do anything when her ass is in heat. When you were in the joint, I didn't let not one nigga put his dick up in this. I'm your lady."

"You right, sweetie. I'm sorry." Capone unbuttoned her blouse. Removed it from her body, along with her black fishnet lace bra. He then unzipped her miniskirt, causing it to fall to the floor. He removed her matching black fishnet panties, and started kissing all around her stomach. He tongued her naval, then gently pushed her back onto the bed, cupped one of her titties and started licking and sucking her nipple, and finger fucked her at the same time.

"I like that, baby," she moaned.

"You do?"

"Oh, yeahhh."

Capone continued aggressively before getting on his knees. He put Night-Night's legs in the buck style and started sucking her pussy 'til she literally started trembling hard all over.

"Fuck me, Capone. Fuck me from the back like you used to do before you went off to prison," she requested, caressing her titties after getting her pussy sucked.

Capone assisted Night-Night in turning over onto her stomach. Then he removed all of his clothing, everything but his socks. He eased back up to Night-Night, grabbed her at each side of her waist while she tooted her ass upward and arched her back, with her legs slightly spread apart. Capone stepped back a moment to peek at her pussy. It was hairy, fat, and wet. The mere sight of it from the back made his ten-inch dick even harder. Night-Night reached and grabbed it. She placed it at her pussy lips and rubbed the head of it around and around it, making herself as wet as possible.

She then allowed him to ease himself inside her. "Ahhh," she moaned, with her mouth open wide and her eyes shut tight. She felt his dick grow bigger inside her. Capone started motioning his dick in and out of her slowly, then around and around.

"That's it, baby. Just like that," she moaned.

Capone worked the middle 'til he found her G-spot. "Oooo, goshhh, baby, yesss. Ah, yes. Fuck me." He sped up his pace, watching her soft ass cheeks bounce off his midsection. "Ahh, God, yes. Hit it, baby. Hit it, hard."

A white creamy foam saturated his dick as he fucked her harder. Night-Night was nuttin' like a muthafucka. Capone felt himself about to do the same. "Damn, baby girl, this pussy gooood," he shamelessly moaned, while at the same time planting himself deep within her.

"That's it, baby, let it go," she said, rolling her pussy around and around as he was releasing himself inside her. "Let it all go inside momma."

"I love you, girl," he said, before he collapsed on her back.

"Don't take it out, baby. Leave it in. Leave it in for the rest of the night," she said.

The following morning, Night-Night awoke to Capone sucking her pussy. He loved fucking in the morning. At first, she thought she was dreaming; that was until he got on top of her with one of her legs over his shoulders and the other spread semiwide. He plunged his ten-inch dick up in her. "Capone," she moaned, squirming up the bed.

"You gon' take all this dick this morning," he said, sticking it to her hard.

"Ahhh, ahhh, Capone, please, baby. Ahhhh," she moaned, looking down at his thick dick filling her pussy. Capone placed both of her legs over his shoulders. "Damn, baby, you want it bad this morning, don't you?"

"Bad as a muthafucka. Throw it to me, Night-Night."

"I wish I could. My pussy's already sore. If you want it you betta get it."

When she said that, he thrust his dick up in her deep, and started pounding her pussy like he was mad. "Like this, Night-Night?"

"Awwwww," she screamed, clawing his ass cheeks with her nails. "Lord have mercy. Goshhh, boy, your dick big."

After Capone finished getting his morning freak on, he went and prepared Night-Night some bathwater. As he washed her back, he saw that her nipples were erect and he was tempted to suck on each of them as he finger fucked her. But he fought it. Other business on his mind overrode his freak inclination.

"Baby girl, while you were asleep last night, I tossed and turned."

"Why was that, Capone? Wasn't momma good to you last night?"

Capone kissed her lips. "Ma, you were damn good to me. You always are. I just couldn't rest. I was thinking heavily on the fact that Tye-Tye couldn't have just killed my brother outside of Fat Jerome's permission."

"You think so?"

"Know so, baby. See, them niggas have a way that they do things. Actually, they are a crew. Fat Jerome is the boss, baby girl. No one in his crew dies outside of his permission, especially when someone of the same crew is responsible for the murder."

"Yeah, but why?"

"I sat up all last night trying to figure that one out. I just know that Tye-Tye didn't just do that shit on his own initiative. That fat nigga sanctioned it. I gotta see him next, Night-Night."

"How you want me to handle it, baby?"

"I can't let you dirty your hands with this one, baby girl. This nigga's mines and all mines."

"What, you gettin' greedy on me, Capone?"

"Got nothing to do with greed, Night-Night. It's about what a gangsta can get away with and what he can't. The nigga who cut my brother's throat, his life is over."

"Damn right it is," Night-Night interjected.

"But the nigga who I believe sanctioned it is still in the city, breathing and having fun. I won't rest until I place my gun in the nigga's mouth and pull the trigger. Now, get dressed, so we can study this enemy."

14

The Prison Library

Derrick had been out of solitary confinement for nearly a year. He was doing his best to keep his word by doing the right thing, staying out of trouble. The majority of his time was spent in the prison library, reading and studying. He had lost his appeal, so he was stuck with doing the sixty-month sentence that he was given. He didn't allow that reality to beat him down. Instead, while attending the prison library on a daily basis, he studied black successful men in the business arena.

Earvin "Magic" Johnson became his number one man to be idolized. He always admired Magic Johnson from the days of Magic being the point guard for the L.A. Lakers. Since Derrick had a few stacks stashed out there in that world, he thought he'd look into the moves Magic was now making as a businessman, in hopes of one

day becoming a successful businessman himself. While he was in the library with his head
buried deep in a *Black Enterprise* magazine,
one of the clerks who worked the circulation
desk approached him. "What's that you reading,
Derrick?"

"Just an article on Magic."

"Magic Johnson?"

"Yeah. Man, the dude's got business sense out
of this world. He gettin' dough like a bakery."

"Can't deny that at all."

"He ain't letting that HIV/AIDS shit stop him
at all," said Derrick.

"Dawg, I know you aren't one of them who
actually believe that Magic has HIV, are you?"

"Hell, what reason would he have to lie about
something like that? Before the whole world at
that."

"He's a businessman, isn't he?"

"Oh, most definitely," Derrick responded.

"A'ight then, there you go."

"Whatcha mean 'a'ight then, there you go'?"
Derrick said, somewhat puzzled.

"You're a pretty smart dude, think about it.
How many people do you know who have HIV
and have lived as long as Magic has? And look as
healthy. Keep it real with me now."

"Dawg, honestly, I don't know anybody close to me who has that disease. So I really can't answer that."

"Well, I can. I had a little brother and an auntie die at the hands of that disease. Seem like the moment they found out they had it, a year or so later the family was attending their funeral. Man, that shit will eat you up quick. You know what it does?"

"What?"

"First, do you even know what HIV stands for?"

"Human something virus, right?"

"Partially. HIV stands for Human Immunodeficiency Virus."

"I was close."

"It's the virus that causes AIDS. And AIDS stands for Acquired Immune Deficiency Syndrome. AIDS, Derrick, is caused by HIV. And dawg, HIV, what it does is it causes the immune system to fuckin' break down, allowing a person with it to get sick."

"That's a meeean muthafucka," said Derrick.

"Damn right it is, bruh. The disease is responsible for countless fuckin' deaths in the black community. Particularly among our black sistas. See, bruh what it does is it invades the T-helper cells."

"What are T-helper cells?"

"T-helper cells are the cells in our bodies that direct the immune system in fighting infections."

"Oh, okay."

"HIV invades these cells, causing them to stop working properly. This is what really causes the body to become extremely sick and weak. A person with this shit not only start losing weight and shit, but also experience fevers, chills or soaking wet sweats, persistent diarrhea. All that type shit. Have you had any of those symptoms since you been incarcerated?" he asked, jokingly.

"Fuck nah. My test results came back non-re-active."

"That's good."

"Besides, dawg, to me, HIV is a damn gay-ass disease."

"So you saying then that Magic Johnson got sugar in his tank?"

"I'm saying the people you see getting that shit mostly are gay-ass muthafuckas. Or fuckin' dopefiends who use dirty-ass needles and shit."

"You got a point. But it's not just a gay disease. That's where you're wrong. Anyone who engages in high-risk activity such as unprotected sex can become infected."

"Yeah. But that shit come from gays, or them niggas on what they call the down low. The niggas on the down low sneak around fuckin' punks and shit, then go back and fuck and infect our women," said Derrick.

"That's true, too."

"And not to drift away from that, but I'm curious as to why you don't believe that Magic Johnson has it?"

"Like I said, a nigga can't play basketball all his life. Niggas get old, you feel me? I think it was a business move, because from how I see it, the nigga would have been dead already. Shit, he got a lot of money, but money can't buy you a new immune system."

"It definitely can help you pay for the type of medicine that can."

"Derrick, man, trust me, when Magic Johnson announced to the world that he was HIV-positive in the very early nineties, there were no real strong drugs that a nigga could take to keep him living as long as Magic has lived with that virus. I think that because HIV/AIDS was hitting hard in the eighties and nineties, and scaring the fuck out of people, that someone as popular as Magic Johnson had to come out and falsely declare that he had contracted it. I think this was done in an attempt to get those who were not spending any money at all on the little medication that was available to start spending money. Because those in the medical arena were losing out. I mean, look at it. No matta what new drug their scientists and doctors could come up with to fight this damnable disease, if no one buys it, not only do they take a hard loss, but how effective the drug actually is would not be able to be determined with true results. Plus, people, particularly black people, once many of them discovered that they had it, and how fuckin' shameful it made them feel, they remained in the closet, electing to not receive treatment. Shit, they knew they were gonna die anyway, because the disease was incurable. Like I said, this thinking caused those in the medical field to lose fuckin' millions. So they fuckin' hollered at Magic, probably offered him a few millions to do speaking engagements and commercials. They knew that Magic had juice in the black community, the community that was being hit the hardest by this shit. Now, nearly everywhere you look, people who have tested positive are receiving their medicines and whatnot and even better medicines have been produced. As a result, those in the medical field are benefiting. It's all business, man. It's all business."

Derrick shook his head in the negative. "I hear what you saying, but personally I don't believe Magic Johnson would lie about his health."

"Dawg, the Bible says it best: the love of money is the root of all kinds of evils. Trust that."

"Well, I still admire the brutha. He's a brilliant entrepreneur. Look at what he has. The man has Magic Johnson Enterprises, a private company that owns more than a dozen twenty-four-hour fitness centers, more than one hundred Starbucks, a T.G.I. Fridays in Los Angeles, and countless movie theaters. The man is like that. You can't take that from him."

"Nah, Derrick, what you can't take from Magic are those championship rings he got as the Lakers point guard. Dawg, that nigga was a beast on the court." After the library clerk said that, some inmate wanting to check out a book called for him. At the same time, the ten-minute move was being announced over the intercom. During the ten-minute move, which was announced every hour, inmates had ten minutes to get to any desired location on the prison compound.

Derrick decided that he'd had enough for one day at the library. So, he headed back to his housing unit. There, he went into his room, lay back on his bunk, and thought heavily on Veronda. It saddened his heart that he hadn't heard a word from her since his confinement. As his eyes watered over the matter, a tear fell down the side of his eye onto the side of his face. *How could she have ever loved me and not stand by my side, or allow me to hear from her at this critical, crucial situational page of my life? I made sacrifices for her. She was my one and only girl, but she rewarded me with sheer silence. What could I have ever done not so right for her to treat me all so wrong?*

15

You Supposed To Be Keepin' An Eye On That Fat Nigga

Capone knew exactly where Fat Jerome laid his head. He remembered going there with his brother Rasco on one occasion, where he remained in the driveway until his brother finished his business inside of Fat Jerome's crib. Sitting in his all-black Cadillac Escalade, with the midnight factory tint on the windows that made it extremely difficult for any passerby to see the faces inside, Capone and Night-Night stalked Fat Jerome, as they had done to one of his top lieutenants, Tye-Tye. From about 200 yards away, they clocked his movements.

So far, all that was visible to each of them was how large this nigga was living. Fat Jerome's home looked like a baby mansion. And it was nothing to see Benzes and other fly-ass rides in the driveway. Only individuals who were doctors, lawyers, or top-notch businessmen and businesswomen resided in Fat Jerome's neighborhood. After three hours of sitting and waiting, a gold minivan pulled up into the driveway. A beautiful missus, along with Fat Jerome, exited the vehicle. Two little girls followed holding each of Fat Jerome's hands.

"For that fat-ass nigga to be a big-ass drug dealer look like he spends quality time with his family," said Capone, looking through his high-powered binoculars.

"Oh, yeah? What you see, baby?" asked Night-Night.

"Him and some fine-ass missus with two little kids. They just stepped out a minivan. You need to stay awake, too."

"She fine?" Night-Night growled. "What's all that shit about?"

"The red chick, thick and cute, Night-Night."

"Negro, don't lay it on too thick, now," she snapped, jealously. "Gon' make me fuck yo' yella ass up in this truck."

"Put it on ice and chill, girl. Now, here, take a look and you'll see what I mean." Capone attempted to pass Night-Night the binoculars. But it was to no avail; she refused to accept them.

"What the fuck I wanna see the bitch for? I couldn't care less about how fine she is. What I look like, nigga, a lesbian? The bitch can't do a damn thing for me."

"You overreacting. The chick can't do nothing for me either."

"You a goddamn liar. The bitch doing something for you: you sitting up in here with a fuckin' hard dick."

Capone couldn't deny his dick was hard as arctic ice. Stevie Wonder coulda seen his thick dick print pressed against his inner thigh.

"What, you wanna fuck her?"

"Cut the nonsense, Night-Night, a'ight?" he said, as he looked back into the binoculars.

"What, you think I'm kidding? I doze off, wake back up, and my man sitting here lusting on a bitch through binoculars with an inflated dick, talking 'bout a bitch fine. What am I supposed to do? Play church girl and stay in my place? Nigga, I don't think so. Now give me those fuckin' binoculars!" She tried to snatch them from his hand while he held them at his eyes, but he moved, dodging her attempt. Unable to grab the binoculars, she grabbed his hard dick and started squeezing it.

"Goddamn, Night-Night! Let my dick goooo. Ouuuch nowwww, that shit hurt."

"It's supposed to. Now, Negro, you supposed to be keepin' an eye on that fat nigga."

"Okay, okay."

"The fat nigga can't be hard to spot, so don't fuckin' play wit' me. You know I ain't the one for that."

"I said okay, baby. You right." She released his dick and at the same time grabbed the binoculars. "Damn, girl, you need to control that jealous-ass temper of yours. No bullshit!"

"Whateva," she said, looking through the binoculars.

"What's going on out there?" said Capone, massaging his dick.

"Fat boy's talking to some nigga who just pulled up in a Corvette. A short brown-skinned cat with shoulder-length dreads.

"Word?"

"Yeah. And here comes your fantasy bitch. She got two pretty little girls with her. They getting into that minivan."

"Who, her and Fat Jerome?"

"Nah. Just the kids. She's talking with Fat Jerome and the guy who pulled up in that Vette. Seems like I know that bitch's face from somewhere, I swear."

"Who, the chick with the two kids?"

"She's the only bitch among the two niggas," Night-Night said, slightly lowering the binoculars only to roll her eyes at him. She looked back through them. "Some other car pulling up now. A silver Honda Accord."

"Who driving, baby?"

"Can't tell right now, hold up. I know where I know this bitch from."

"Where?"

"A picture. That nigga, Tye-Tye. She was on a big-ass picture with him. The bitch had the same damn hairstyle: a French wrap."

"Word, baby?"

"Fuck yeah. I got a photographic memory. I don't forget shit."

Capone thought a moment, and then it dawned on him. That chick was the mother of Tye-Tye's girls. He forgot all about Tye having twin girls. The chick and li'l girls weren't Jerome's family.

"Remember the car I just said pulled up? Well, a dark-skinned girl just got out."

"Let me see."

Night-Night passed the binoculars to him. "Oh, that chick," said Capone. "That's Ericka. Ericka James. She used to strip in the clubs and shit."

"Really?"

"That ho ain't nothing but a slut. She'll fuck any nigga with money and a dick."

"You crazy. What you think she doing over at this nigga's crib?"

"Shit, I don't know. Your guess is as good as mine. Probably over there to suck the nigga's dick."

"A nigga that damn fat can't have much of a dick to suck, shittt," joked Night-Night.

Capone laughed. "You're a clown, girl," he said. "I see the chick with the two li'l girls pulling off in that minivan. The nigga in the Corvette pullin' out, too. I should follow the chick."

"For what? So you can find out where she live and try to fuck her later?"

"Night-Night, cut the nonsense for real now, a'ight, before I smack the damn shit out of you. Enough is enough."

"Whateva."

"I don't know why you trippin' anyway, shit. I'm with you every damn day. Twenty-four muthafuckin' seven. So what time would I have to do any fuckin', huh? But you can't see that far right now because the fog of your jealous-ass spirit has blurred your vision."

"Like I said, whateva. It was you who got fuckin' aroused. So for real, Capone, don't mess with me with that. Furthermore, I'm through with it. Matta fact, take me back to the hotel."

"Oh, so now you wanna leave me?" asked Capone.

She didn't say anything. Instead, she poked her lips out, looked out the window opposite Capone, and shook her head from left to right. Capone could see from the side of her face that her eyes were getting watery. "Noooo," she said in response to him questioning her wanting to leave, her voice was breaking up. "You . . . you just act like I ain't enough for you." Her tears broke him down. He hated seeing her cry for any reason.

"C'mere, baby," he said, putting the binoculars down and wrapping his arm around her neck as he leaned sideways. He tried to kiss her on the side of her lips, but she put her hand up to prevent it.

"No. Go on, Capone," she responded.

"Night-Night," he said, grabbing her by her hand and holding it with a firm grip, "don't do this to me, now. You're more than enough for me, baby. I fuckin' love you. You're all I damn got."

She pulled her hand from his with force. "Well, don't be getting all aroused off of other bitches then. You can control your nature a li'l better than that. That's all I'm saying. That shit is disrespectful and you know it. Shit, if I was getting all wet and horny from checkin' out a fine, fly-ass nigga your ass would have a fit. I know you," she declared. "Now tell the truth, wouldn't you?"

"You got that," he conceded. "You right like a muthafucka."

"I know I'm right."

"It won't happen again, baby, okay? I promise it won't happen again."

Night-Night reached inside her purse and pulled her 9 mm out. She placed it underneath her leg. "It betta not, or I'm blowing somebody's dick off. Now pay attention to that fat nigga's movements before you miss something," she said.

Capone licked his lips, eyed her, and then slid his hand between her inner thighs. Night-Night was wearing an Apple Bottoms jean skirt. He rubbed up and down her inner thigh.

"When it comes to you, fuck Fat Jerome. I don't wanna miss you. I missed you for three years and some change while I was in the joint. That alone was hell," he said. His gentle touch made her panties wet. She gapped her legs semiwide. When she did so, he maneuvered her panties to the side with his finger and started massaging her clit while at the same time looking through the binoculars. What he was doing felt so relaxing and good, she placed one of her legs on top of the dashboard, closed her eyes with her head cocked back on the seat's headrest and allowed him to finger fuck her 'til her anger from her jealousy subsided.

The time was passing swiftly like an eagle moving toward its prey. It was now a little after eight in the evening. Capone and Night-Night had stopped spying on Fat Jerome to go get a bite to eat. When they returned, they noticed that Ericka's silver Honda Accord was still in his driveway. The clouds were forming and flashes of lightning after the sounds of booming thunder appeared like tree roots across the sky. Little drops of rain began to wet the earth's surface. The earth in certain parts of Charlotte wasn't the only thing getting wet. So was Ericka's pussy inside of Fat Jerome's home. Fat Jerome had called her and requested she come over so that the two of them could talk business, which involved her riding to Atlanta with Osama to locate Veronda. Also, he had wanted to put his dick in something.

"That's all you want to do, Fat Jerome, is the nasty?" Ericka asked, as she paraded around in Fat Jerome's den in nothing but an all-white thong. She had removed everything else from her body, per Fat Jerome's request. It was something she couldn't deny him. Neither for his pleasure, nor hers. The last time he called her over to his crib to get his freak on, he bought her a brand spankin' new Honda Accord, the one that was currently getting her where she wanted to be and needed to be in the city.

Hopefully this time will be rewarding as well, she thought, as she seductively walked over to him. He was sitting on the edge of his black leather sofa set. She turned around with her ass in his face, bent over with her legs spread, touched her toes and started making her ass cheeks shake like they were being electrocuted. Her ass cheeks looked so soft as they shook in his face, he couldn't resist putting his face between them.

He told Ericka to open her ass cheeks while she bent over.

"With my thong on?" she inquired.

"No, take your thong off."

She removed her thong. "Now, turn back around, bend over and spread your ass cheeks," he instructed. Ericka did so, gripping her ass cheeks to spread them as wide as she could. She spread them so wide she could feel her asshole open. Fat Jerome licked up and down her hole. Then he made his tongue wet and stuck it directly in her asshole and started circling it.

"Oh, goshhhh," she gasped. "Lord knows you're so awesommmme." This was the first time Fat Jerome had tongue fucked her asshole. No one had done it before him. He stiffened his tongue and motioned her hips back and forth with each of his hands, while she played with her clit. "I'm . . . I'm . . . I'm c . . . cummin', big daddy," she uttered. After she got hers, Fat Jerome reached for his K-Y Jelly and covered his dick with it. Ericka looked on curiously.

"What you doing that for, big daddy?"

"Because I wanna fuck you in your asshole."

"My asshole? I ain't never been fucked up my ass."

"Don't worry. Don't big daddy always take care of you?"

"Yeah, but shit, I ain't never let a nigga put his dick up my ass."

"It won't hurt, Ericka, baby, I promise."

Ericka thought on it for a second or two. *What if this nigga bust my li'l asshole open and mess me up for fuckin' life?* She then looked down at his dick, which she knew he had fuckin' low self-esteem about, being that it was so damn small. It couldn't have been any longer than four, or five inches. It was thick, though, like a dill pickle. *Maybe it won't hurt. The nigga's tongue sho' felt good. Maybe his dick'll feel even better. Fuck it. I'ma let his ass fuck me. But I ain't taking all of his thick li'l dick at once. Fuck that!*

"What you want me to do, big daddy, sit on it?" she asked.

"That's all. Now c'mere," he replied, with lust in his eyes, stroking his dick.

Ericka stepped to him and turned around. Her heart was beating fast as hell. She grabbed a hold of his dick, which was saturated with K-Y Jelly. She put it at her asshole and eased down on it. She took only the head of it first.

"See, that's it, Ericka," he said, cupping her titties, while she moved up and down on the head. "Oooo, yeah, ride big daddy's dick. It feels wonderful in ya, don't it?"

"It . . . it feels good as hell," she replied. She then started getting into it as her asshole adjusted to the size of his dick. She started grinding down hard on his dick and twirling her ass around and around, taking all of it.

"That's it, Ericka, baby, this yo' dick. Work it, baby, work it."

She bounced up and down on it as if she had forgotten all about the fact that this was her first experience with a hard dick up her ass. Fat

Jerome started spraying all up in her. She felt her ass get wet and heard Fat Jerome breathing hard as hell as if he was having an asthma attack. "You all right back there, big daddy?"

He squeezed her titties, the both of them with each of his hands. "Girl, Ericka, you got the best asshole I ever put my dick in. Grab those set of keys on the table over there. They're the keys to your new crib, a condo I got for you off Independence. Damn, girl, you know how to throw that ass. I told you if you be true to me, I'll be true to you."

"Damn, big daddy, I appreciate this shit," she replied, with more excitement and awe in her voice than a sissy in a roomful of big dicks.

"That's nothing," said Fat Jerome. "But looka here, I'm gonna need for you to make that trip that I was telling you about over the phone."

"The trip to Atlanta with Osama, right?"

"Precisely."

"I gotcha, big daddy," she said, looking down at him once again stroking his semi-erect dick.

"That bitch Veronda gotta pay," he uttered, before Ericka grabbed a wet towel that he had nearby on the sofa and wiped his dick clean. She then got down on her knees, gripped his hard dick, and started sucking and licking on it.

In the midst of her sucking the hell out of his dick, she looked up at him. "I'm not Veronda. I could never betray you, big daddy. She's my girl and shit, but she always been for her fuckin' self. Plus, she always thought that she was better than me. Little did she know, I secretly hated her for that shit, you know?"

"I don't even want to think about the bitch while you're making me feel good. Momma, you're the best, no bullshit," he said, while she deep throated his dick and simultaneously massaged his balls. "I'm fuckin' making a lot of money out here. I don't have time for petty bullshit," Fat Jerome said, running his hand over Ericka's hair.

Ericka let up off his dick, pushed him backward onto the sofa, and then got on top of him. "Do you have time for this, big daddy?" She placed his dick inside her hot, wet pussy and started riding it.

"Girl," Fat Jerome uttered with his eyes damn near closed from the pleasure he was receiving, "you know I'm crazy as fuck about yo' slim black chocolate ass. It is true what they say."

"What's that, big daddy?" she said, moving up and down his dick at a snail's pace.

"The blacker the berry, the sweeter the juice."

"You think so, daddy?"

"Precisely, baby girl, because everything I need, you're giving it to me right now. Every gangsta need a chick like you in his corner to ease his street stress."

"Oh, certainly, big daddy. Certainly."

1:00 a.m. . . .

"Baby. Get the fuck up and look at this shit!" shouted Capone, holding his binoculars with one hand, and shaking the arm of Night-Night with the other.

"Huhhhh?" she uttered, awaking from her brief slumber. "What is it, Capone?"

"Not what is it, Night-Night. Who is it? That should be your question."

"Well, who is it?" she said, looking through the binoculars. Her vision was somewhat blurred from having her eyes closed for the past hour.

"Look over to your right. You see that all-white Crown Victoria parked over there on that corner?"

"Yeah, I see it. Who is that? One of that fat nigga's partners?"

"Fuck no, baby. Them the muthafuckin' feds."

"Say what?"

"Damn right! They just pulled up about thirty fuckin' minutes ago that I noticed."

"They got this nigga under surveillance too, huh?"

"You betta believe it. That's why we 'bout to bounce," said Capone.

"Let's do that then," concluded Night-Night.

16

Maybe He Doesn't Give A Damn About Me

While in Atlanta, things were going semi a'ight for Veronda. She had copped a one-room apartment, more like a townhouse, on the west side; a candy apple red used but decent 2007 Honda Civic; and an upgraded wardrobe. One thing she quickly understood was that niggas in the ATL loved the fuck out of chicks who could fuckin' dress. She was making niggas freeze in place like she was an ice-cold breeze when they would get a glimpse of her in something like a full-body Baby Phat skintight skirt that just barely covered the bottom of her ass cheeks. Shit like that she wore in the summer months. In the winter, she busted them niggas asses with tight-ass Levi's jeans with the matching jacket and shirt. She always wore thongs so that her ass cheeks could bounce and shake hard in her jeans. Damn near everywhere she went, whether to a McDonald's trying to cop a Big Mac and fries, or to a gas station simply bending over to pump her own damn gas, when niggas got a good look at that booty of hers, they would sweat her like a muthafucka for a date.

One dude had gotten so caught up in her beauty on one occasion while she was exiting a beauty salon that he walked straight up to her with five one hundred-dollar bills in his hand. He twisted his body in a slick, pimpish fashion. "Yo, excuse me, miss. I know that I don't know you. Nor you me. But I swear before heaven and earth that I will give you all five of these one hundred-dollar bills if only you would allow me the pleasure of suckin' your pussy."

Veronda distorted her face in a manner that went from glamour girl to straight fuckin' ghetto. "Nigga, what the fuck I look like, a prostitute?" she snapped.

"Nawww, sexy. Not at all. But you do sure as hell look good enough to be on someone's breakfast plate. It's still early. How 'bout it, huh, sexy?"

"Man, pleeease. You got some nerve to even step to me like that," Veronda said, getting into her car.

The nigga couldn't handle being rejected. "Fuck you then, you stuck-up bitch. Your pussy probably stank anyway."

Oh, no, the fuck he didn't. She got out of the car after removing a .25 automatic gun from her purse. She hid it in the back pocket of her jeans.

"Nigga, ya momma's pussy stank," she shouted.

"What the fuck you say, bitch? I know you didn't say something about my momma," he retorted, walking toward her with a mean facial expression like he was gonna smack the fuck out her ass. That's when she reached and retrieved her gun from her back pocket.

"Don't walk up on me, nigga," she said, making her gun visible. The sight stopped him in his tracks. "Now, nigga, I didn't disrespect you initially. You disrespected me," she said.

"Okay, okay, ma'am. You right, I was wrong."

"You goddamn right you were wrong. I ought to bust yo' ass for not knowing how to conduct yourself in the presence of a woman when you see one."

"Look, miss, I was wrong. I'm sorry. Matta fact, here." He dug into his pocket, balled up the $500 he had offered her earlier and tossed it at the roof of her car, nervously. He then backed up and started running.

"Punk-ass nigga, got me fucked up," Veronda said to herself, as she got back into her car and zoomed off. After Fat Jerome had disrespected her, she made up her mind that no nigga was ever gonna mistreat her in any fashion. She even quickly rid herself of the fear of guns, realizing that while out in this cold-ass world where disrespect is a common thing, a person without a gun was bound to get run over.

Veronda didn't even dare date a man while in the ATL. She had been there damn near a year and some change. No dick had touched her pussy, only a dildo. She didn't trust men anymore after that li'l incident with Fat Jerome. Plus, she was saving her loving for Derrick. She had hoped that by now, Derrick would have traveled to ATL to see about her. But such hoping produced no fruit. She tried writing to his mother, but had discovered that his mother had moved. Every letter she wrote was sent back to her. Even Derrick's cell phone number had been disconnected. *Maybe he doesn't give a damn about me after all,* she thought, almost to the point of tears, for she deeply loved Derrick.

She wandered through her apartment before checking her stash. She realized that along with the $500 she was given earlier by that punk-ass nigga she encountered, all she had was about a grand left. The reality of the situation made her contemplate going back to doing what she knew best: strippin'. Strippin' was something she had embraced years ago as a teen after she had run away from home. She'd been on her own ever since. But when she was sixteen, she was at home one evening with a girlfriend of hers who was two years older than her.

The two of them were in Veronda's bedroom when Veronda's stepfather had come in from work. The first thing her stepfather noticed when he stepped foot inside their house was how outrageously loud Veronda's stereo was blasting. She was playing R. Kelly's "Bump N' Grind." When Veronda's stepfather got upstairs and approached her bedroom door to knock, he noticed that he didn't have to because her bedroom door was cracked open. What he saw stopped him in his tracks. Veronda and her friend were buck-naked. Veronda was lying on her back being dildo fucked by the hand of her friend, who was also licking her clit. Veronda had absolutely no awareness at all of her stepfather's presence at her door. Neither did her friend.

Veronda's stepfather saw that her eyes were closed tight and her hips were gyrating with the dildo that was buried up in her deep. And although her stepfather couldn't hear her over the loud music, he knew that she was moaning because her mouth kept opening wide. As he went unnoticed by either of them, he viewed their naked, young, healthy bodies. More so Veronda's friend's than hers. The sight left him with a massive hard-on. From the angle that he was standing at the door, he could clearly see Veronda's friend's body from the back. Her ass cheeks were juicy and firm. Her hairy bush was poking out nicely as she was bent over on her knees, satisfying Veronda with her tongue and that dildo. Veronda was cupping and squeezing her titties. For a moment her stepfather thought that perhaps he was dreaming.

There was no way his stepdaughter was a bisexual, he reasoned. But when he concluded that what he was witnessing was in fact real, he realized not only were his eyes not playing tricks on him, the dick that was solid hard in his pants wasn't either. It was literally throbbing. He, therefore, unzipped his pants, released his hard dick, and started masturbating. He had gotten so caught up in the act of watching Veronda and her girlfriend freakin' while he masturbated that he failed to notice Veronda's mother making her way upstairs to tell Veronda what he intended on telling her before he was stopped in his tracks.

"What in the hell you doing?" she shouted.

He hardly heard her. But the expression on her face told him that his ass was busted. He tried putting his dick back into his pants, but it was so hard and long that doing so became difficult. He saw her coming his way angrily, so he went inside Veronda's room. Veronda and her friend were caught by surprise. And neither one knew what to expect, seeing him with his hard dick in his hand.

Her mother shortly followed. Her seeing Veronda and her friend naked with a dildo on Veronda's bed was more of a shock than seeing her husband with his dick in his hand, masturbating. Veronda's mother immediately turned the stereo completely off. She saw Veronda reaching for her panties and bra. So was her friend. Her husband had by now put his dick back into his pants.

She looked at him and smacked the hell out of his face. "You son of a bitch!" she snapped. "You ought to be ashamed of yourself. Got ya dick out watching them like you don't have a wife." She smacked his face again, this time harder than the first.

He stood there speechless and holding his face. "Baby, please, I can explain."

"There is no explaining. Get the fuck out of my house, nigga! And you, Miss Grown Ass, what the hell you call yourself doing?" she shouted between hitting Veronda with her fist.

Veronda felt embarrassed, and she wasn't about to take much more of those licks from her mother. Her mother was heavy-handed and her licks hurt. "Momma, you ain't got to hit me like that," Veronda said, frowning before her mother cut her off.

She struck her again. "You are not grown, young lady," her mother said, hitting her some more in rage.

Veronda started crying. At that point she became so angry that she jumped in her mother's face and started wildly swinging. When her mother continued her assault on Veronda, the two of them tore that room up, fighting.

"No, Veronda, please don't fight your momma," Veronda's friend shouted.

She and Veronda's stepfather got between them. Veronda had scratched her mother's face up badly. And Veronda's mother had busted Veronda's nose and lip. Blood was all over Veronda's face and parts of her body.

"You can't stay here," her mother said, breathing hard. "Getcha shit and bounce. 'Cause if you think you gon' lay up in my house, you and this here lesbian chick, you are definitely mistaken."

"Whateva, Momma," Veronda shot back, wiping her bloody nose with a T-shirt.

When Veronda said that all sassy-like, her mother broke away from her husband's grip and started beating her ass again. "I don't know who you think you talking to, but I will beat the goddamn shit out of you in here," she snapped. It happened so fast that all Veronda could do was grab her mother's hair. Again, Veronda's girlfriend grabbed her while her stepfather grabbed her mother.

"The two of you getcha asses out my house and don't ever come back," Veronda's mother said, as her husband dragged her out of Veronda's room.

"Get yo' hands off me, son of a bitch," she said to her husband on her way out of Veronda's room.

That was the last time Veronda stepped foot in her mother's house. She had rather stayed in the streets than return to the house of the woman who beat her like she was an enemy. "Fuck that," she had said to herself. She then began rippin' and runnin' the streets doing what she could to survive. Had she not been so pretty, she probably would have starved. Her beauty got her to strip in clubs. And strippin' in clubs opened up doors for her to meet ballers, who opened up doors for her to hustle drugs and other little things before she met Derrick.

Now, in need of fast cash once again to pay her bills in the ATL, she went to her closet and started pulling out her different Victoria's Secret lace bras and matching thongs in hopes of doing what a girl gotta do to survive.

17

Report To The Lieutenant's Office

On the prison's recreation yard in Edgefield, SC, where Derrick was serving his time, bruthas had their shirts off, getting their rec on. Niggas were sweating up a river under the rays of that hot-ass ball of fire ninety-three million miles from the earth called the sun, as they played basketball, jogged on the track, or lifted weights. Doing those activities helped bruthas doing their time rid themselves of the stress of the many years that many of them had to serve. Those activities also helped bruthas keep their asses in shape, physically. Coupled with getting much rest, those activities were the reasons most bruthas, when they got out, looked far younger than others their age who had not experienced prison life.

The bruthas who were not somewhere on the recreation yard getting their rec on were more than likely in the chapel, library, or just straight in the dormitory, sitting in front of a television. Derrick was inside his dormitory room, preparing to go outside and play basketball. He was hoping to do so with the express intent of sweating thoughts of Veronda from his mind. Constant thoughts of her well-being and her not keeping in touch wore on his mind so heavily that it had started becoming extremely difficult for him to do his time in a peaceful state of mind. While getting his recreation clothing together, he thought on something he heard an older prisoner say to another.

The older prisoner had said, "If a chick don't write her man while he is in prison, doesn't visit him, or doesn't do any damn thing that her ass is supposed to do for him that's an indication that she has moved on with her life and, as a result, has essentially said through her actions, 'fuck him!' Such a chick has embraced another dick. Wasting precious time thinking about her and trying to bring her back to a place she never should have left, which is by her man's side, especially absent a legitimate explanation, is worthless.

"The truth is, itching pussies have to be scratched. And these bitches' asses are so hot these days that if some nigga didn't pour water on them, their ass would burn up. That's why I never trust a bitch, especially one who's slick and of the streets, to do time with me. My bitch was as slick as they came, which is why after I received those thirty-plus years that the government gave me, I told that bitch to get the fuck on. She was crying and shit, talking 'bout, 'I love you. I ain't never gonna leave you.' Man, I broke down and gave that bitch the benefit of the doubt and guess what? That bitch crossed me like Eve crossed Adam. I hadn't been locked up a year when I called home and another nigga answered that bitch phone. Man, I was pissed like a mutha-fucka. Here it is a bitch I had taken out of the ghetto and treated her ass with such royalty that niggas thought her ass was straight out the suburbs. When that bitch was with me, she ate the best foods, went to the best places, and wore the finest linen. Yet I can count on one fuckin' hand how many money orders the bitch done sent me.

"That's why niggas in here have to let them bitches go until they fuckin' come to their senses and realize that they can search and search, but they'll never find real-ass niggas like those of us in here who tried to do fuckin' right by their asses."

Those words from the older prisoner that Derrick had overheard stuck with him. Although when he first heard the older prisoner talk like that, he thought the old man was just bitter. But now after not hearing from Veronda at all, he was beginning to believe the words of that old man. He headed out the door to play some ball, but before he could get far, the dormitory correctional officer stopped him.

"Derrick," he said, "report to the lieutenant's office."

"Report to the lieutenant's office?" Derrick repeated, puzzled. He knew that whenever an inmate was called to the lieutenant's office it was either to be piss tested for dirty urine or to be served a disciplinary write-up.

"Yep. The lieutenant just called for you to report to his office immediately."

"Did he say what for, sir?"

"You know they don't tell us all that. Just one of those cases where you find out once you get there," the officer replied.

"Dammit, man! Jackin' a nigga's rec," Derrick snapped.

"What was that, Derrick?" asked the officer.

"Just talking to myself, man, shit. Tell 'im I'm on my way. I gotta change my clothes and grab my ID."

Derrick entered the lieutenant's office approximately ten minutes after his dormitory officer had
spoken to him. He was escorted into a designated
room. Sitting there were two white individuals:
one male, the other female. Both of those individuals had nametags attached to their upper
clothing. As Derrick got closer, the two individuals stood up in unison. At that moment, Derrick
knew who they were. They were both FBI agents.
He just didn't know why the fuck they were in
Edgefield to see his ass.

"Hi, Mr. Derrick Bellamy. I'm Agent Amy
Williams," she greeted him, with a smile and her
hand extended. Next to recognizing her badge at
her waistline, he noticed that she was a redhead
with freckles all on her face. Derrick embraced
her hand with a strong, firm shake. He did so
more out of courtesy than because she was a fed.

"And this here is my partner, Agent Jonathan
Haymaker." Agent Haymaker bowed his head
slightly and extended his hand. Derrick shook
it, looking him directly in the eyes. He noticed
Agent Haymaker had a long visible scar on the
left side of his face, like a nigga had put a razor
on his ass in the past.

All of them took their seats and Derrick spoke.
"I'm puzzled," he said. "Two FBI agents here to
see me. I must be in some type of trouble. If so,

then please allow me the opportunity to at least phone my attorney."

"Mr. Bellamy, you're not in any trouble," said Agent Amy Williams.

"Please, call me Derrick, it's fine."

"Well, Derrick, like I said, you're not in any trouble—"

"I heard that part, now give me the other part," he said, cutting her off.

"I'm gonna be straightforward with you, Derrick."

"I'd appreciate it."

"A small-time dealer we just busted a couple weeks ago by the name of Eric Brunson, aka 'Eric B.,' happened to make mention of your name."

Derrick folded his eyebrows in disbelief. "My name was mentioned? What the hell do I have to do with this Eric B. getting busted? I mean, why did my name surface?"

"Mr. Brunson did not bring your name up in a manner that would incriminate you in any way."

"Are you telling me that Brunson is an informant?"

"What we are saying, truthfully, is your name came up and we want to ask you a few questions about a very well-known drug dealer in Charlotte and surrounding areas. We have had this guy under surveillance for some time now. His name is Jeremiah Jerome Jenkins, aka 'Fat Jerome.'"

Derrick shook his head slowly in the negative. "I have never heard of him," he lied.

Agent Amy Williams looked over at Derrick with serious doubt in her eyes. Before she could express that doubt, her partner spoke up, seeing that Derrick was about to play hard on them. "Derrick, no offense, but how much time do you have left on that sixty-month sentence the judge gave you?"

"Y'all the feds, man. I'm sure you know."

"You're right. You've got about three more years to do, because in the federal prison you do eight-five percent of the time."

"Okay, there it is. Now what?"

"We know that you know Fat Jerome. My partner and I reviewed some surveillance tapes and discovered you coming out of a pool lounge in North Charlotte with him. Let me tell you what else we know. We know that your mother has discovered that she has breast cancer. And, Derrick, whether you know it or not, your little brother has drifted into the streets. He's now hustling crack on the west side where you used to hustle and—"

"Man, that's bullshit and you know it," Derrick snapped, cutting him off.

"Which part? Your mother having breast cancer or your little brother hustling crack?"

Even though Derrick had no idea of his mother's situation, his little brother selling crack on the corner troubled him the most. "My little brother's damn near a genius in school; there's no way he's selling coke."

Agent Haymaker motioned for his partner to pass Derrick a manila folder that she had on top of the table in front of her. "Feel free to take a look inside, Derrick," said Agent Haymaker. His partner folded her hands and rested her chin on them as her elbows rested on top of the table. She watched Derrick look in the folder and pull out the two pictures that were inside.

What he viewed was not only enough to anger him, but it was enough to make his eyes water to the point of wanting to cry. Since he was in the company of strangers, he restrained himself from shedding a tear. What he was beholding were two pictures of his little brother, Mike-Mike, on the block, serving drugs to someone in a car. Derrick stared at the two pictures long and hard. He couldn't believe it.

"Derrick, that person inside that car, accepting those drugs from your little brother, that guy is an undercover agent," said Agent Haymaker.

"Then why didn't they bust him?" Derrick inquired.

"Because we aren't interested in juveniles. We're interested in Jeremiah Jerome Jenkins."

Derrick pushed the folder across the table to agent Amy Williams. He then hit the table hard with his open palm. "Shit!" he said in anger.

"Now, Derrick, please don't get upset," said Agent Amy Williams. "We—"

"Don't get upset? That's my little brother in those pictures. What you mean, don't get upset? Wouldn't you be if you were in prison, trying your best to do the right thing, while the only brother you have, who is damn near a genius in school, is out there doing the wrong thing?" snapped Derrick, cutting her off.

"I know where you're coming from, Derrick, that's why if you scratch our back we'll scratch yours," she assured.

"What do you mean by that?"

"Look, I'ma be straight with you, Derrick," Agent Amy Williams said. "We can cut a deal with the U.S. attorney's office to have you out of prison in less than a week if you help us nail Fat Jerome."

"Help y'all, huh? What you really mean is become a rat for the government, right?"

"We call it helping yourself."

"Well, Mrs. Amy Williams, I'm no snitch."

"I never said you were."

"You all got my files. You know what I'm in here for. I am here for nothing more than a simple gun possession violation."

"Yes, we know that," she replied.

"I took my time on the chin like a man. No codefendants, no bringing any hustler down to soften the bed I made and now have to lie in."

"We understand that."

"Furthermore, I could walk out of this room right now and get stabbed completely to death if the wrong person got wind that I was in here being visited by two FBI agents and giving someone up to them. Truth is, the streets don't honor hustlers who can't hold their water. Neither do the true convicts who are in here doing thirty, forty years and even life sentences because of stool pigeons. I'm accepted in prison by these types of convicts because my legal papers reveal a standup guy. Now you want me to tarnish that and become a rat. Well, I don't think so."

Agent Amy Williams had been an FBI agent for nearly fifteen years. Every prisoner she ever questioned with regard to another hustler being investigated always played hard. One out of twenty usually got away with it. Mainly because that person had been through the system, knew how it worked, and for whatever other reasons would simply not cooperate under any circumstances with law enforcement. Agent Amy Williams didn't see this type of guy in Derrick's eyes, although he was displaying a hard thuggish persona. "Look at me, Derrick. I want you to look me in my eyes and tell me truthfully that you would rather give a damn about holding on to a hardcore street personality than be in a position to not only be free, but perhaps save your little brother."

"That's what you don't understand, ma'am. It's not about being hardcore; it's about honoring a code of the streets."

"Honoring a code of the streets? There is no honor among thugs, Derrick. In fact, one of the definitions of a thug is cutthroat. Guys out there in those streets don't care anything at all about you. It's every man for himself out there."

"Well, that's just your opinion."

"That's not just my opinion. That's a fact. Most of the guys we bust want to be the first to cooperate. They know that once those indictments start coming back from that grand jury most of them will be facing some pretty lengthy prison terms and nobody wants to spend forever behind bars, not for coke or gun possession, nor to protect some person hustling out there in the streets who probably don't even love them. Some guys even call us from prison, asking us can they now cooperate, because after doing a few years they see that their so-called friends whom they were loyal to haven't returned the favor. Some of them tell us that their so-called friends don't write them, don't send them money for commissary, don't even go by and drop a few bucks on their kids. Nothing!"

"I can't speak for everybody. But none of my hustling friends have mistreated me since I've been incarcerated. Even if they did, I would deal with them once I regained freedom," Derrick said.

Agent Amy Williams continued to try to persuade him. "Do you feel Fat Jerome loves you?"

"Doesn't matter," Derrick replied.

"Do you love your little brother and your mother?" Agent Amy Williams asked.

"You can believe that more than you believe in the good Lord above. I love my family with a passion."

"Then why don't you help us, Derrick, so that you can get back to them? Like I said, we just want you to help us nail Fat Jerome, whom we have been building a case on for nearly five years. But just when we think we have witnesses who are gonna testify, they end up changing their minds, or they end up dead."

"What makes you think that I won't end up dead if I decide to cooperate?"

"We can't say. All we can say on that is, if you decide to help us, we can hide you out in a witness protection program, where we would have to change your identity. In that situation, you would not be allowed to have any contact with your family or friends whatsoever."

"I can't go out like that."

"However, if you don't want to do it that way, then what you can do is just keep a very low profile until we arrest and detain him and his crew. But I promise you that if you cooperate with us on this case, we will have you out of here in a couple days."

"A couple days, huh?"

"A couple of days. You can bank on it."

Derrick started pulling hairs from his chin. There was nothing he wanted more than to be out of prison and home with his family. He had missed them dearly since he'd been incarcerated. The year and a half that he had now been incarcerated seemed like forever. With three more to do, coupled with both his mom's and little brother's situations, he felt that maybe it was time to compromise the street code.

"I tell y'all what." Derrick scooted up in his chair. "If you can have me out in a couple of days as you said you could, I promise I will tell you everything I have ever done with Fat Jerome and I'll come to court to testify, fuck it!"

The two FBI agents looked at each other then offered their hands to Derrick. He shook their hands. "Guess we'll be seeing you in a few days then," Agent Haymaker said.

"I guess you will. We'll see," Derrick concluded.

When Derrick left the presence of Agent Haymaker and his partner, Agent Amy Williams, he felt dirty. The very last thing he wanted to do was become a stool pigeon on someone. Even though he didn't like Fat Jerome, potentially working for the feds to nail him was something he had to think long and hard about, even after having given his word already to both agents that he would cooperate. He even thought about praying on the matter and asked himself, "What would Jesus do?" But then it hit him: Jesus was crossed by someone who associated with him, Judas. *There was no way Jesus would sanction crossing another person.* So he shook that thought off and decided that life is what it is and that sometimes you just gotta do what the fuck you gotta do!

18

Strippin'

"Girl, I'm 'fraid," said Veronda. "It's been a minute now since I last done this."

Veronda was in the ladies' dressing room, preparing herself to go on stage. So was the girl she was conversing with. The girl was a twenty-seven-year-old blonde, blue-eyed stripper whose stage name was Pink Tale. Pink Tale was sitting at Veronda's left, powdering her nose in the big mirror they both were looking through.

"How long is a minute? Two, three, four years?" inquired Pink Tale.

Veronda thought a moment. "Mmmm, it's been about two good years. I need the money though."

"Shit, girl, that's not really long."

"Yes, it is too," said Veronda, picking through her hair.

"If you say so. But I feel you on the money thing. Shit, I need it too. Bush got the economy all fucked up!"

"You ain't lying. Barack Obama and his administration gon' fix it though," said Veronda.

"Shit, I hope so, 'cause I just got laid the fuck off from a job that I've been working at for the last seven years."

"What were you doing?" replied Veronda.

"Working at a check cashing place down in Decatur. I was only strippin' part-time."

"So you strip full-time now, huh?"

"Got no other choice. Hell, bills gotta be paid and a girl's gotta eat out here."

"Oh, no doubt about it. Like I said earlier, I need the money my damn self. I just don't know if I still got it."

"Stand up, Veronda," said Pink Tale.

"Stand up?"

"Yeah. Stand up."

Veronda stood up. She saw Pink Tale eyeing her body from head to toe.

"Okay, now turn around and make your booty shake."

"Girl, are you serious?"

"Hell to the yeah. Now do it. Do it just like you would if you were onstage before a crowd of horny-ass men."

Veronda turned around and started making her ass cheeks shake.

"There you go, girl. Shit, you still got it."

Veronda started blushing. She slightly hit Pink Tale on the arm. "Girl, Pink Tale, you're a mess, I swear." Veronda then sat back down to finish putting makeup on her face.

"Where are you from anyway, Veronda?" Pink Tale asked, looking at Veronda through the mirror.

"Charlotte, North Carolina."

"The big Queen City, huh?"

"Yep. They ought to call it the Mean City."

"Why you say that?"

"'Cause niggas there don't know how to fuckin' treat a woman. You start letting niggas get a li'l bit of you-know-what."

"Mmmm, hmmm."

"And they start wanting to mishandle a girl, you feel me?"

"Girl, do I. Dudes down here the same way, a lot of them. Prime example: I was being kind one night by giving a dude a private lap dance in one of the VIP rooms. Usually, I just do my thing on stage, get my money, then go the hell on about my business. But there was this particular player who begged me to give him a VIP session. He told me that it was his birthday and that he would be leaving for the military the following week. Well, I reluctantly went into the VIP room. I only was wearing a see-through fishnet bra and a short-ass skintight skirt with no panties."

"No panties?"

"I know, right? But after I had come off stage, the panties I had on were so wet from the performance that I just came up out of them."

"Okay, well, go 'head."

"Me and this birthday cat was in that VIP room. I was giving the nigga the lap dance and show of his life, and he was putting hundred-dollar bills all in my bra. Then, all of a sudden, the cat grabbed me from the back and pulled me to him, aggressively. He was strong as hell, and before I knew it, I was on my back with my legs open and he was putting his dick up in me, while at the same time holding my arms down. Veronda, girl, I swear this cat had the biggest dick I had up in this li'l tight hole of mine. He bust my shit all up."

"Didn't you even scream?"

"Shit, yeah! I tried, but fuckin' nobody couldn't hear me because the club music was so loud. And when he finished fuckin' the hell out of me, he looked me straight in my eyes. 'If you tell anybody about this, I'll find you and kill you.' Shit, the way that nigga's eyes looked into mine, there was no way I was taking any chances running my mouth about that. I walked around with a sore pussy for a week straight."

"Damn, girl."

"You the only person I ever told that. So see I know how mean these cats can be. That's why now I don't go anywhere without this." Pink Tale reached into her purse and pulled out a blue steel .38 revolver.

When Veronda saw it, she said, "Girl, I know that's fuckin' right. I got my ass a gun too. I used to be afraid of 'em, but not anymore."

"Now if a nigga try that shit again like that Mr. Birthday Boy tried, his ass gon' have so much lead up in him people gon' think his ass is a pencil," said Pink Tale, before she and Veronda heard a knock on the door. Then they saw the nightclub owner enter.

"Veronda, you're up next," he said.

"Okay, here I come." When the nightclub owner stepped back out, Veronda got ready. She then looked over at Pink Tale. "It was nice meeting you, Pink Tale," she said.

"You too, Veronda. By the way, don't you have a stage name?"

"Yeah, it's Venom."

"Okay, Venom. Well, try not to put too much in 'em out there. Shit, save some for me."

"Oh, don't worry; they won't all be dead when you get to the stage. I promise."

Veronda approached the stage, wearing a plain Jane–ass candy apple red satin bathrobe. Underneath it she was wearing a candy apple red lace bra and matching fishnet G-string panties, along with the candy apple red spaghetti-strap stiletto heels. She noticed that her audience was silent as she stood on stage with her back facing them. But as far as she could see from when she entered the stage, the club, which held about 700, was jam-packed with nothing but ballers and playas.

The lights were dim in the club. The only true visible light was the one that was shining on Veronda as she stood motionless on stage. Her heart was beating fast. She took a deep breath in hopes of relaxing. She then held out her arm and snapped her finger, giving the DJ the cue to play her favorite song, "Chopped N Screwed" by T-Pain. The DJ honored her request and her song began blasting through the club's high-amped speakers.

Veronda started doing the butterfly while at the same time disrobing. The moment her robe fell to the floor and the playas and ballers alike got a glimpse at how fat, firm, and juicy her ass cheeks were they all started barking like they were dogs in heat. She then bent all the way over, gripping her ankles, and started wiggling her ass cheeks, while looking at the facial expressions of her audience through the split between her legs. Her pussy lips could be seen from the back as she bent over. This sight alone was enough to make niggas throw twenties and fifties at her feet. She turned around, cupped and squeezed her tits, and danced her way to the hand that she saw holding up the most cash. Surprisingly enough, it was a lesbian chick with her tongue out as if to say, "I will suck that pussy of yours dry if you bring it my way." Veronda didn't discriminate. The money was all she was there for, regardless of who had it. She began rolling her pussy in this lesbian's face, enough for the chick to throw Veronda a crispy hundred-dollar bill. That wasn't enough though. Veronda wanted the whole damn stack this chick had in her hand. Therefore, she got directly in the chick's face and sat before her on stage with her legs open wide. Nothing but Veronda's fat, shaved pussy could be seen in her G-string. The lesbian chick started winking her eye and licking her lips.

Veronda leaned back on both her arms and started twirling her pussy around and around. Her pussy was so close to this lesbian's face and lips that the lesbian took her chances and pulled Veronda's panties to the side and started licking her clit. Veronda allowed her to do so, while damn near everyone in the club looked on. The lesbian chick danced up and down and around Veronda's clit with her tongue. Veronda welcomed the heavenly feeling as much as her audience welcomed the sight of her pussy being exposed to this lesbian chick's tongue. She continued twirling her pussy in this lesbian chick's face until the stack of cash that was in the chick's hand was finally inside Veronda's G-string panties. She backed up from Veronda and then winked her eye while simultaneously licking her lips. Veronda blushed and started making her way to the nearest baller, who also was holding up a lot of cash in his hand.

She made her way to him, dancing and cupping her titties. She squeezed them, then turned around and made her ass cheeks wiggle hard as she slightly bent over in this baller's face. He reached out and spanked one of Veronda's ass cheeks. Her ass cheek was so soft it bounced like a basketball when he spanked it.

"You bad as a muthafucka, momma," the baller shouted, before throwing three fresh fifty-dollar bills at her feet.

To thank him, she blew him a kiss. She then made her way off the stage, picking up all the cash from the stage that she had so graciously earned. As she made her exit, she turned back to her audience one last time, waving her hands and blowing kisses. She left the dogs barking and it had paid off fairly well.

When she got home that night, she discovered that she had made almost $4,000. The stack the lesbian chick gave her alone was $3,200. She noticed on one of the hundred-dollar bills that the lesbian chick had written, CALL ME TONIGHT, CELL# 961-0880. Veronda debated whether to call this chick. First of all it was late, two thirty in the morning to be exact, and she was tired. Furthermore, this lesbian chick had briefly licked Veronda's clit so damn good that had she not pulled away when she did, Veronda would have found herself nuttin' like a muthafucka right there on stage. This frightened her. She just wasn't quite ready to be sexually locked down, even though this chick's tongue felt so good touching her most sensitive flesh.

As she contemplated whether to give the chick a call, she heard a very unexpected knock at her door. She grabbed her gun and placed it in the back pocket of her jeans. She had no idea who or what awaited her as she went to answer.

19

Cooperating

Exactly four days after Agent Amy Williams and her partner, Agent Jonathan Haymaker, visited Derrick in prison, they had him out as promised. His first destination as he rode home, escorted by them, was to their office. There, Derrick cooperated with them. He told them of all his dealings with Fat Jerome. He signed sworn statements stating that all that he had in fact revealed to them was true, and that he would testify to it when the time came.

When he left their office under the strict recommendation from the both of them for him to keep a low profile, the only thing that seemed to matter to him was seeing his dear mother and confronting his little brother about what the FBI agents had shown him. He, therefore, took a taxi to his mother's new address.

Damn, this a nice-ass neighborhood, he thought, seeing the clean streets and the big, beautiful houses. He then saw something that snapped his ass out of his amazement at the sight of his new neighborhood. He saw his candy apple red old-school Chevy Impala parked in front of his mother's car. He was amazed that his car still looked good and that the chrome on it had not dulled as far as he could see.

"How much do I owe you, sir?" Derrick asked the taxi driver.

"Thirteen dollars and twenty cents."

Derrick handed the man a twenty dollar bill. He then awaited his change.

"Here you go, young man. You have a beautiful day now ya hear?"

"You too, sir," replied Derrick before exiting the taxi.

He didn't even get good on his mother's porch before she came running out to greet him. "Oh, my Godddd! Derrick, why didn't you let me know that you were being released today?"

"Just wanted it to be a secret," he said, hugging her tightly.

She placed both her hands at each side of his head where his ears were and looked him in his eyes, then up and down. "Baby, you look so good. I missed you."

She hugged and kissed him again, before they made their way inside. "So how do you like our new place?" she asked.

"It's beautiful, Momma. It really is," he said somewhat sad.

His mother looked at him again in his eyes. "Boy, Derrick, you got those big, pretty light brown eyes just like your daddy. I can look at them and tell when something is heavy on your mind. What is it, baby? Aren't you happy to be home? God knows I'm happy to see you."

Derrick saw that his mother had lost about fifteen or twenty pounds. She always was slim, but now she looked as if she had been up day and night on crack. She had a bandanna on her head and, when she hugged him both times, he could feel that her strength was failing her.

"Momma, why didn't you tell me?" he asked, avoiding her question of whether he was happy.

"What, Derrick?"

"About the cancer."

She turned away from having direct eye contact with him, then grabbed her feather duster and started dusting off the top of the television.

"Didn't I deserve to know, Momma?"

"You had enough to deal with, being incarcerated and all."

"You are the only mother I got. What if—"

She cut Derrick off and stopped dusting. "What if what?" she said, repeating his question. "What if I would have died while you were in prison? That's neither here nor there. The only thing that matters is I'm still here. I thank God every day for that. I know I look a little different, but I'm getting better."

"So, are you on chemo?"

Derrick's mother removed her bandanna so that he could see that her hair had been shaved. She then said, "What this tell you?" He looked at her clean-shaved head, and his eyes started watering. His mother saw that and shook her head. "No," she said to him, "don't cry, I'm fine." A tear dropped from his eye anyway as he went to wrap his arms around her.

"I missed you," he said, "and I deeply love you. I ain't never leaving you again, Momma. I promise you that." She wiped his face with her hand.

She then said, "I thought I told you, Derrick, to never make promises you can't keep."

"No, Momma, I can. And I will. I'm through thuggin'."

"If you are through thuggin', son, and trust me, you ought to be, that means God does answer prayers."

"Yes, He does answer prayers. I just hope that He answers the one I got, and restores your health completely."

"He will. But don't stop praying until you see results. Because God don't always come when we want Him to, but, Derrick, He is always on time. Always."

"I know. Look at our new place. That couldn't have been the work of no one else but God," said Derrick.

"Well, your room is down the hall to your left. And Mike-Mike's is right across from yours. I was gonna take the room across from yours, but Mike-Mike insisted on being directly across from you. That boy love him some you."

"And I love myself some him."

"You ought to go to his school, Derrick, and surprise him. He'll be so glad to see you home."

"Think so, Momma?"

"Mmmm, hmmm. I gotta go to work. You know I still do housekeeping for the doctor lady. She's so nice. She's the one who gave us this house."

"Wow!" he said, even though she'd already told him that.

"Mmmm, hmmm. And didn't charge me a thing. She said all of the years I worked for her she has been wanting to do something special for me and my kids. She said it was the least she could do, seeing that I have been so faithful to her. That's why, Derrick, son, it pays to be kind to others. If you plant good seeds in life, that same good will eventually return to you. The same goes for if you plant bad seeds."

Derrick's mother continued dropping her wisdom in his ear. When she finished, she went and prepared to head to work. "Momma, are you sure that you should be working and not resting?" Derrick said as his mother was about to walk out the door.

"I'm fine, son," she replied confidently, "I done rested up enough, trust me."

"If you say so, Momma. I love you."

"Just stay out of trouble. You know it's easy to get into, but hard as hell to get out of."

When Derrick's mother exited the house, he briefly had two thoughts running through his head. He thought on how extremely blessed he and Mike-Mike were to have a mother as strong as the one his mother was. He never knew her not to be a black woman who didn't stand her ground. She was his first example of what it meant to not let anything in life stop you from doing what was right. Derrick, however, chose the thug path to follow, and knowingly chose to sell drugs. He was beginning to see that what was right was honoring his mother.

He would never sass her again. He used to feel that the only reason she was coming down hard on him was because she needed a man in her life. Since his father's death, Derrick never once saw her with a man. Derrick had felt that maybe her needing one in her life could perhaps cure her of getting in the way of him thuggin' and doing what he wanted to do. But now after having a little time to think about life and his overall situation with his family, he saw that his mother didn't need a man at all. All she needed was what she already had an intimate relationship with her Lord and Savior Jesus Christ.

Next to Derrick thinking hard on this, he thought hard on his stash. Before he had gotten arrested, he had been keeping the savings from his drug money in a secret compartment located in his car underneath his dashboard on the passenger's side. The former drug dealer Derrick bought his car from had told him about the secret compartment that he had made for the sole purpose of stashing drugs.

Derrick hoped that when his mother went to retrieve his car from the police station no thorough search of it had been conducted, and that when he would go to check, his money would still be there.

He waited until he figured his mother was good and gone, grabbed his car keys from her dresser's top drawer, and went out to his car. He jumped inside and tried starting the engine. The engine turned, but not completely over. He continued trying while simultaneously patting his foot on the gas. Finally, the engine turned over completely and his motor started running. "That's my baby," he said, talking to his car.

He then retrieved one of his old-school CDs. It was N.W.A.'s *Straight Outta Compton*. It was pumpin' hard as hell through his Kenwood speakers. He had only been home a few hours, but hearing his rap music and inhaling through his nostrils the smell of his car's leather seats made him know for sure that he was back on the muthafuckin' bricks in the free world. Nonetheless, because of his new neighborhood, he purposely turned down the volume on his music. The last thing he wanted was the neighbors running to his mother, talking about her son disturbing their peace and shit with his loud music.

He checked his surroundings before checking his stash. He did so more out of hood instinct than anything. In the hood somebody was always sneaking around and shit, trying to check out what a nigga was doing. The coast was clear.

With that understanding, he reached to check for his stash. He reached his hand far underneath his dashboard until he felt plastic. That was all he had hoped he'd feel, a sure sign that all was well and intact. He retrieved it, and uttered a brief prayer after looking it over.

"Thank you, God, for not letting them crackas find my money." Then he opened the plastic Ziploc bag and pulled it from one of the stacks wrapped tightly with a rubber band. He put it to his nose and took a whiff. "Yes, indeed," he said to himself out loud. "Only in America."

He left his car running while he got out only to go inside to put his money up in his bedroom closet. After doing so, he jumped back into his car with absolutely one other thing on his mind: paying a visit to Mike-Mike's school.

20

I'm Michael Bellamy's Older Brother

Derrick remembered that Mike-Mike's school let out at approximately three o'clock. It was two thirty when he got to the schoolhouse. He bumped into a tall Caucasian male English teacher. Derrick stopped him and mentioned the name Michael Bellamy, which was Mike-Mike's real name. "Ah, yes," the English teacher said, "Michael Bellamy should be in Mrs. Taylor's math class right now."

"I appreciate it, sir," replied Derrick politely.

"No problem at all. Mrs. Taylor's classroom is exactly four classrooms across the hall. That one right down there," the English teacher said, pointing his finger in the direction of the classroom.

"Thanks again," Derrick said, before moving toward the classroom.

Derrick stepped to the classroom window where he viewed the class. He looked for his little brother, but didn't spot him. *His li'l ass must be sitting way in the back somewhere in the corner.* Mrs. Taylor saw Derrick at the door and went to greet him.

"Sir, I saw you looking through the window at my class. Is there something I can help you with?"

"Yes, ma'am. I'm Michael Bellamy's older brother."

"Oh, you must be Derrick?"

"That's me. How did you know that?"

"I've walked up on Michael writing you letters while he was supposed to be doing his class work. When I took one of his letters, I discovered that he was writing not only someone who was in prison at the time, but someone who was his brother. That boy talks about you all the time."

Derrick smiled. "Well, that's definitely good to know. I really missed him while I was away. I had to leave because I got myself into a little trouble."

"At least you're home now. And hopefully, you're home to stay. However, Michael hasn't attended my class in two days. In fact, I was gonna call his mother today to see if he was sick or anything, because I really miss his classroom participation. He is such a bright kid."

"I'm gonna see what the problem is, ma'am, and hopefully you'll be seeing him back in your classroom soon."

"I surely hope so."

Derrick left the school campus, burning up inside that his little brother wasn't in school where he was supposed to be. He was hotter than a furnace ignited by gasoline.

Where on God's green earth could my brother be? Derrick thought as he drove his car. Then it hit him. The pictures! The pictures that the FBI agents had shown him of Mike-Mike on the corner, selling crack.

Derrick headed straight to the west side, and lo and fuckin' behold, there was Mike-Mike on the damn corner, alone with some other kid. Mike-Mike couldn't see Derrick's car pulling up about half a block away because his back was turned. Derrick hoped that he would stay like that.

Derrick parked his car and started speed walking toward Mike-Mike whose back was still turned in the other direction. Neither Mike-Mike nor the kid with him saw Derrick approaching. But once Derrick was in arm's reach of Mike-Mike, he grabbed him by the back of his collar aggressively.

"What in the fuck are you doing on a mutha-fuckin' corner? Huh?"

When Mike-Mike saw that it was Derrick, every part of his body started trembling. "Bruh, I . . . I didn't know you were home."

"And I didn't know that you had been skipping class just so you could sell dope."

"Who the fuck is this cat, Mike-Mike?" asked the kid who was with him. The kid was about sixteen years old. He lifted his shirt to expose the butt of his 9 mm.

Derrick turned Mike-Mike loose and walked up on the kid slowly. Once he was in arm's reach, Derrick said, "What is it to you who I am, huh?" Before the kid could say anything, Derrick reached and snatched the kid's gun. "I ought to shoot you in your fuckin' face."

"Please, Derrick, bruh, he didn't mean any harm," interjected Mike-Mike.

"Shut up and wait for me in the car."

Mike did as he was told. He didn't want to make Derrick any madder than he already was.

"Now, you get on your knees, young thug, since you bad and wanna show me your gun and shit."

The young kid got on his knees. "Man, I apol-ogize," he said.

"Fuck that," said Derrick. "Open your damn mouth. Open the muthafucka!"

"Man, please don't shoot me," the kid said. Tears started flowing down his face. "Please, man, I got a mother and it'll kill her to hear that her baby boy was gunned down."

"You didn't think of that when you lifted your shirt and showed me your gun like you was some type of bad-ass gangsta. Now did you?"

"I was just looking out for my friend Mike-Mike, that's all. Please, man, don't shoot me."

"I tell you what, get your ass up and run home. And I betta never see you out here on this corner ever again. Do you hear me?"

"Yes, sir."

"Now get up and run home." The young kid did exactly as Derrick had informed him. The kid took off in such a hurry that Derrick saw him nearly stumble and fall. That's not all Derrick saw. He saw a cop rolling two streets over. Derrick tossed the gun nearby and left it in some bushes and started walking toward his car. As he was walking toward his car the cop pulled up next to him. Derrick knew that he was about to be going back to fuckin' jail. *Shit,* he shouted within himself. But to his surprise the cop kept it moving until he was completely out of sight. Derrick wiped the beads of sweat from his forehead, jumped into his car, and drove off.

"Whether you are a friend or a foe, sister or a brother your actions in this world will certainly affect others."
—K. Tomblin

21

How The Fuck You Get Yourself Involved With Selling Drugs?

Derrick drove straight home with Mike-Mike on the passenger side. He was so heated that he didn't allow his mouth to open up to utter a word to his little brother.

All Derrick could seem to do, other than think about how bad he wanted to beat Mike-Mike's ass out the frame, was clench his teeth together hard and turn up the volume on his Keyshia Cole CD, *The Way It Is,* in hopes that his anger would somehow subside.

Mike-Mike didn't say shit either. His ass was too afraid to do so. All he could do was think about how Derrick would scold his ass. He knew it was coming. He also knew that there would be nothing his young ass could do about it.

"Getcha ass in the house; and make no mistake about it, I'm right behind you," Derrick said to Mike-Mike as he put his car in park at their house. He needed a minute alone to cool down before going in behind his li'l brother. When he got into the house, he found Mike-Mike coming from the bathroom, zipping up his pants. He got directly in Mike-Mike's face. "How in the helll did you get yourself involved with selling drugs, Mike-Mike? Riddle me that? And you betta not lie to me. I'm telling you!"

"Momma, bruh," Mike-Mike replied.

"What you mean, Momma?" snapped Derrick.

"Momma, bruh. She needed money for medication. So I pretended that I had gotten a job after school at a car wash off West Trade Street. I just wanted to help her, Derrick, bruh, that's all."

"You think you were helping her by selling fuckin' drugs?"

"She was sick and even started losing her hair and whatnot. I felt compelled to do something. I didn't really want to, but I figured if you were here then you probably would do the same thing."

"How the hell you figured what I would do? Huh?"

"I just did, bruh."

"Well, let me tell you something, you're not me. Therefore, you don't know what I would have done."

"You're the one who told me that the reason you were hustling prior to your arrest was because you were trying to get us out the hood."

"And?"

"So I figured that if you would sacrifice going to college just to sell drugs to help us get a home of our own, I felt that helping Momma get her medication was a good enough reason for me to do it."

Derrick wanted to punch Mike-Mike in his damn face for thinking like that. "Look, you got your own mind, Mike-Mike. And you know right from wrong. I always have told you that selling drugs wasn't the way. That I didn't want to be out in these streets."

"Yeah, bruh, but you wasn't here to see Momma suffering."

"It doesn't fuckin' matter! You know fuckin' right from wrong. Now don't you?"

Mike-Mike dropped his head.

"No, don't drop your head on me," said Derrick. "Answer my damn question. Don't you know right from wrong?"

"Yeah, I do."

"How old are you, Mike-Mike?"

"Going on fourteen years old."

Derrick took a deep breath when Mike-Mike said that. "You are still a baby, little bruh. You think Momma is sick battling cancer now? Imagine if she would have somehow found out you were on a goddamn corner selling crack while you should have been in school? To hear that would literally kill her. Now tell me, who the fuck gave you drugs to sell? Matta fact, empty your pockets." Mike-Mike did as his brother ordered. He removed drugs from one pocket and money from the other. Derrick held the little bag of drugs up to his face. "How much coke is this?" he demanded.

"About four hundred dollars' worth," Mike-Mike replied.

"And how much money is this?"

"Nine hundred, maybe."

"Is this all the drugs and money you got? Don't lie to me either."

"I got more."

"Where?" asked Derrick.

"In my room, underneath my bed, in my Nike shoebox."

"Go get it all, right now."

Mike-Mike retrieved the coke and cash he had in his shoe box and gave it to Derrick.

"How much coke and cash is this supposed to be, Mike-Mike?"

"Two ounces of coke and thirty-five hundred dollars."

"Who the fuck gave you this coke?" When Derrick asked that question he noticed Mike-Mike hesitating in giving him an answer. Mike-Mike remained silent like he was under arrest. This made Derrick extremely mad. He hit Mike-Mike in the back of his head with his open palm. "Did you not hear what the fuck I asked? Who the fuck gave you these drugs?" Mike-Mike knew if he didn't answer, the next lick he would receive wouldn't be an open palm at the back of his head. It would be a fist straight in his face. He definitely didn't want that. He knew that Derrick was heavy-handed, and that a fist from Derrick in the face would leave him disfigured.

Rather than suffer that fate, Mike-Mike said, "Eric B. gave them drugs to me."

"Eric B.?"

"He told me not to tell you, Derrick."

"Told you not to tell me?" Derrick repeated. "You wanna know why he didn't want you telling me that shit? Because he knows that I disapprove of giving you drugs to sell. And that I would put a bullet in his brain for sure if I found out he gave them to you."

"I know, bruh, but—"

"But my muthafuckin' ass! I have done every-thing to ensure that you avoid walking in my footsteps. But I go to damn prison a little while, come back home, and what do you know, my damn baby brother's hanging out on a fuckin' block like he knows what the fuck he's doing."

"Like I said, Derrick, I didn't want to."

"Don't matta! You ended up doing it," Derrick retorted, cutting him off. That's when both of them heard the phone ring.

"Hello?" said Derrick, answering the telephone. It rang four times, interrupting the conversation he was having with his little brother.

"This is a collect call from the Mecklenburg County Jail in Charlotte. This call is from Eric Brunson."

Derrick accepted. "Yeah!"

"Yo, who dis? Little Mike-Mike?" asked Eric.

"Nah, nigga, this Derrick. And—"

"Oh, shit! What up, my nigga?" he greeted him, cutting Derrick off.

"Fuck that, man," Derrick snapped. "What the fuck you doing giving my little brother drugs?"

"Ho . . . hold on, Dee, bruh."

"Ain't no fuckin' hold on, nigga! What you did is a violation, Eric B., and you know it."

"Look, Derrick, I was only trying to help out, that's all."

"Help out?" Derrick repeated him, hotter than a ball of fire.

"That's all, man. Yo' li'l brother told me about the situation with your mom and how she was taking chemo or something like that. He said that he wanted to help her get her medicine, so I was like I'll give her the money on the strength of Derrick, 'cause Derrick's like my brother. That's what I was doing at first. But, Derrick, dawg, I got tired of lying to your mom. When I would give her a few dollars for herself and some to send you, she would be like, 'Where you know Derrick from? And what do you do for a living to have lots of money all the time?' I would tell her that you and I went to school together, and that my father is a successful real estate investor in upstate New York, who sends me cash on a regular. That was all I knew to say. But, man, your mom isn't an easy woman to fool. She used to give me a look that read, 'You doing the very same thing that my son Derrick was doing: selling them drugs.' The only reason I think she allowed herself to take money from me a few times was because she couldn't prove what I had shared with her was actually a lie."

"Regardless of that, Eric, why did you give my li'l brother drugs to sell? That's what I'm fuckin' upset about, dawg."

"Again, on the strength of lovin' you like a brother, I would come over and scoop li'l Mike-

Mike up sometime and take him to the Bobcats games and whatnot. He used to always be fascinated with my fly-ass clothes and kicks. You know how we do it, Derrick."

"Man, just get to the point," said Derrick, feeling his patience wearing thin.

"Well, he straight came out and was like, 'Eric, man, I wanna hustle. My brother gone and my mother is on chemo. I need some money and I don't want you giving it to me. I want to earn my own.' Man, Derrick, those are the words of your li'l brother."

"So you let those weak-ass words convince you to give him some work?"

"Man, shit, if I didn't give it to him some other hustler would've."

"That's a fucking lame-ass excuse, dawg, and you know it. Just tell me that your own fuckin' greed got in the way of you making a fuckin' intelligent decision."

"It had nothing to do with greed, dawg. Look, man, you were in the joint with sixty months to serve. And for real for real, your little brother was feeling your absence in more than one way. And you gotta realize, Derrick, these youngsters out here are just like we were when we wanted fast cash. Just like we were determined to get it however we could and from whomever we could, they are the same way. That's the way it is, dawg," said Eric B.

"It doesn't make a difference how you see it, Eric. I can't forgive you for giving Mike-Mike drugs to sell. And let me just tell you why. First of all, he ain't even fourteen years old yet. He's a fuckin' kid, literally. Secondly, he doesn't have any idea as to the dangers that lurk on dem corners. You and I both know that there are niggas out in them streets who will roll up on you, put a jimmy to your head, and rob you for all your coke and cash. But not just that, Eric. Them crazy niggas aren't the only ones out there that have to be watched out for. The cops out there, too. They are the biggest threat to any illegal hustler."

"You definitely right about that," replied Eric B.

"You damn right I am. And you fuckin' know what? When them damn feds came to that prison where I was doing my time, they told me you mentioned my name. Not in an incriminating way."

"I just wanted to help you get out of prison."

"I ain't trippin on that. Besides, I'm home, ain't I?"

"Definitely."

"And I only told them about Fat Jerome. Fuck that bitch-ass nigga. However, that's neither here nor there at the moment. But you know what those federal-ass agents showed me?"

"What's that, Derrick?"

"Them muthafuckas showed me two goddamn pictures of my fuckin' little brother selling crack to an undercover agent."

"Fuck nah," said Eric B. in disbelief.

"Nah, fuck yeah! 'Cause it was real. I wanted to flip the fuck out after I beheld those pictures. Those pictures helped me make the decision to make a deal with the feds, 'cause for real for real, rattin' ain't my thing. But, dawg, I went back to my cell in that prison with mainly one thought that I just couldn't seem to shake. Who in the hell is the nigga who gave my little thirteen-year-old brother crack-cocaine to sell on a corner?"

"If it means anything, Derrick, man, I apologize. Looking back now, I see that I wasn't thinking. Bruh, please don't hold it against me. I love you like my own brother."

"Just know that the drugs my little brother still have of yours is in my possession now."

"I ain't trippin' on that."

"And the money, too."

"Again, Derrick, man, I ain't trippin'. Just as long as my and your relationship isn't affected to the point of not being able to forgive one another."

"I might forgive you in time. But, dawg, I ain't gon' ever forget."

When Derrick said that, an operator came on letting Eric know that he had one minute left to talk.

"Look," he said to Derrick, "these crackas got me on trafficking charges."

"How much?" asked Derrick

"A kilo of crack and half a kilo of powder."

"So, what they gon' do?"

"Try to fuckin' throw the book at me."

"Okay, and?"

"And I'ma fuckin' cooperate. I got to, dawg. Shit, it's that or twenty to life."

After Eric made that statement, Derrick heard a dial tone. Eric's time had run out.

Derrick hung up the phone and spotted Mike-Mike coming out of the bathroom, zipping up his pants again. Derrick looked at him madly. "Head back into the bathroom and I'm on my way behind you." When both of them were there, Mike-Mike saw the cocaine Derrick had in his hand. "You see this shit?" Derrick demanded as he began pouring it all down the toilet. "I betta never ever catch you with this shit in your possession again. You are not a fuckin' drug dealer.

You hear me? Your ass is gonna go to school and be some damn body, or I'ma put a bullet in your head. And I ain't bullshittin'. Now have I ever lied to you?"

"No."

"Then you believe what the fuck I just said to you more than you believe our momma got cancer. 'Cause I meant what the fuck I just said."

Having made the trip to Atlanta, Ericka and Osama left a hotel they had checked into and went straight to Veronda's apartment. It was about 11:23 p.m. according to Osama's watch. While they were on the highway, Osama told Ericka to call Veronda from her cell phone. Ericka hesitated. She then said, "Fat Jerome told me not to call her at all once we got to the ATL. Those were his exact words, Osama."

"He told me no such thing. Besides, why would he?"

"He said he just wanted me to show up and surprise her and then you would come and do your thing."

"Well, Fat Jerome isn't here. And I'm the one who's gonna take care of the business up here. So, give her a call like I said."

Ericka started dialing Veronda's number. She wasn't gonna question Osama by any means. Shit, the way she felt about it was if she got out of line with this crazy-ass nigga he probably would leave her ass in Atlanta, deceased.

That's just how Osama was. He was the quick-tempered, no-nonsense type of nigga. He really didn't want to travel to Atlanta with Ericka beside him from the start. He felt women were fuckin' weak when it came to street business. And as a result of that, he didn't appreciate her company. He knew that once he got his hands on Veronda it would be over for her. Him knowing that was one thing; Ericka's ass knowing it too was another. That's what troubled Osama when Fat Jerome told him that Ericka would be riding with him to Atlanta.

Fat Jerome knew that Veronda knew Osama's face. So, to relax Veronda, he would use Ericka, whom Veronda had been keeping in contact with off and on since she'd been in Atlanta. Ericka had Veronda's address and everything. She would be the perfect individual for the setup.

Osama liked doing things solo. He believed no witnesses, no snitches! However, he reluctantly went along with Fat Jerome's plan.

Ericka finished dialing Veronda's number. Her phone rang five times before Ericka heard her answering machine: "Sorry, I am unable to come to the phone right now, but if you would leave a message, I will be sure to get back atcha fo'sho."

Ericka folded her cell phone, disconnecting her call. "Nobody's answering her phone," she said to Osama.

"Well, shit, try it again until somebody answers."

Ericka did as she was told, but got the same results every time. Finally, they pulled up to Veronda's apartment. "You stay here, Osama, while I check to see if she's home," said Ericka, before getting out the car. She approached Veronda's door and hit the doorbell. She waited for someone to answer. But no one ever did. After fifteen minutes of waiting, she and Osama went back to the hotel, disappointed as a muthafucka.

While at the hotel, Ericka kept trying to reach Veronda, but there was nothing. Absolutely nothing. She ate some pizza that she and Osama had delivered to their hotel room. As she did so, she watched Osama wipe down his gun. It was a 9 mm with a specially made silencer, a tool designed for one thing: killing without anyone hearing a sound.

22

You Mind Washing My Back?

Ericka decided that she would take a shower and go to bed, after not being able to reach Veronda all night. All she could seem to do was reach Veronda's answering machine, and she got sick and tired of hearing that same damn recording over and over again. She let the warm water from the shower relax her as she thought about her gift. *Fat Jerome bought me a muthafuckin' condo out there off Independence Boulevard, where them rich-ass crackas at. That nigga loves this pussy.* She exited the shower with her head wrapped in a towel as well as her body.

She figured Osama was asleep in the other bed. They had a double. So, she didn't come out of the bathroom with any panties on. Truth was, she had forgotten she had them on her bed in her luggage bag, along with her bra. When she exited the shower and entered back into the area where her and Osama's beds were, the lights were out, but the television was on. Osama was not asleep. In fact, he had put his gun away and had removed all of his clothing with the exception of his boxer briefs, patiently awaiting her exit.

"I didn't know you were still awake, Osama," Ericka said. He grabbed a pair of underwear from his bag and walked to the bathroom. His dick was swinging from left to right in his boxer briefs. *That short-ass nigga got a big-ass dick,* Ericka thought before hearing him respond to her.

"I couldn't go to sleep without washing my ass. You washed yours, didn't you?" he asked, then entered into the bathroom and turned on the shower. Ericka sat on her bed and dried herself completely off. She then put on a pink wife beater shirt, and a pair of matching Victoria's Secret panties. She was about to get underneath the covers and call it a night until she heard Osama shout, "Ericka, could you please come here a minute?"

Please come here? Ericka repeated to herself. *Shit, I didn't think his gangsta ass had any manners.* She made her way into the bathroom where she saw his body completely soaped up. "You called me?" she asked rhetorically.

"Yeah. You mind washing my back? I can't reach it."

You mind sucking my pussy? Ericka said to herself before saying, "Nah, I don't mind." Ericka soaped the washcloth and circled his back with it. She started at the top of his back then made her way down.

"That feels so good, Ericka, I swear it does."

"I know. I'm getting wet all up again by this damn shower water," Ericka said.

"Stop crying. It ain't nothing but water."

While Ericka was continuing to wash his back, she sneaked a peek at the dick that she saw the print of while he had his boxer briefs on. Sure enough, it was just as she imagined it was, nice and big. "Osama," she said, while circling his back with the washcloth, "may I ask you something?"

"Anything. Go ahead."

"Do you have a lady?"

"Nope."

"And why would that be? I mean, you're short and handsome with these long dreadlocks."

"All that doesn't matter. That's the physical. I'm too into the streets to have a lady," he said, cutting her off.

"Oh. I was just curious," she said, handing him his washcloth and looking at his dick.

He saw her eyes when they went down south at it. And when she turned to leave, he noticed that she looked real sexy in her li'l bikini pink panties. He felt his nature rising and wanted to say, "Ericka, come back here so that I can fuck the hell out of you right here in this mutha-fuckin' bathroom before I put on my boxer briefs for bed."

But then he remembered just what he was in the city of Atlanta for. He was there on business, but after drying off, when his hard-on didn't subside, he felt that maybe a good fuck wouldn't hurt anything at all. He left the bathroom with only his boxer briefs on. His dick was poking outward from not being able to get Ericka's sexiness out of his head. He looked and saw Ericka reading a book, lying on her stomach. She had no covers on her body at all. He noticed that although Ericka was slim, her ass looked fat in her panties.

"You reading in the dark, Ericka?" Osama asked.

"It ain't that dark in here. The light from the television is fine."

"I heard a long time ago that reading without sufficient amount of light will fuck your eyes up."

"That may be true for some. But hell, I been doing it damn near all my life and ain't shit

wrong with my eyes," she responded, while at
the same time turning around to lie on her back.
That's when she saw Osama placing his dirty
underwear in his bag. That wasn't all, though.
She peeked from the side of her book and saw
his dick poking outward.

To her it looked every bit of eleven to twelve
inches. She loved herself some big dicks, and
even though it had been awhile for her since she
last had one, she started feeling herself getting
moist between her legs at the sight of Osama's
dick. She had only been fuckin' Fat Jerome
lately. And it didn't take a fuckin' rocket scientist
to be able to tell whose dick was the biggest
between the two of them. Osama's dick made
damn near three of Fat Jerome's dick as far as
she could clearly see and she wanted some of
it just like he wanted some of her. Without any
procrastination on her part, she put her book
away. "Osama, will you reach in my bag down
by my bed and get that baby oil and rub it on my
back for me, please?"

"No problem," Osama replied, surprised as a
muthafucka to hear her ask him what she did.
He definitely wasn't gonna contest by a long
shot. He retrieved her baby oil and watched her
roll over on her stomach.

"Wait a minute," she said. "Let me take off my shirt." She removed her shirt, thereby allowing Osama to get a quick glance at her nice-sized titties. Ericka had Foxy Brown titties. She lay back on her stomach and enjoyed Osama's touch. He started at her shoulders. He gently massaged them, then her back. He ran his hands, saturated with her baby oil, up and down her back.

"Mmmm, Osama, that feels great," she moaned, not taking into consideration at all that his hands were hands that killed people. The lust she had for the dick wouldn't allow her to.

"Does it?" he replied.

"You can put me to sleep just with your hands. Oooo, Goddd yess," she replied.

Osama continued pleasing her with his massage. When he got to her lower back, he rubbed and massaged more intensely. "Yes, that's it, Osama. That feels good." Osama's dick was literally throbbin' inside his boxer briefs. And Ericka's panties were wetter than the shower she and Osama both took. Osama stopped a moment. He did so to place more baby oil onto his hands. He glanced over at her booty. Ericka's pink panties were fitting tight. One side of them was even wedging in her ass. If he didn't put his dick up in her, he knew that he would have to jump in bed and just fuckin' masturbate. He was at his peak with lust for her goods. So he decided he'd step his game up. Instead of placing his oily hands on her back to continue massaging it, he grabbed each side of her panties and proceeded to ease them down.

What the hell took this nigga so long to remove my fuckin' panties? Ericka tooted her booty upward so that he wouldn't have any problem getting her panties off. He then started massaging each of her ass cheeks with each of his hands. "I thought I said massage my back, Osama," she said playfully.

"You did," he replied, squeezing her ass cheeks. They were so soft they felt like cotton in his hands.

"Then why are you massaging my booty?"

"The same reason you allowed me to ease your panties off. I wanna fuck. I ain't even gon' front."

And I wanna make love. She then turned her body over, thereby, stopping him from massaging her. "You wanna fuck, huh?" she asked. She saw him get up from the bed and remove his underwear. His dick popped forward like it was a jack-in-the-box. He then stood before her. From the light of the television she could see that his dick was stone hard. She reached for it, gripped and moved it back and forth, then started playing with his balls.

"That's it, Ericka, damn all the talking." She allowed him to continue standing while she sat up in the bed, only to have his dick meet her mouth. She sucked on it a little at a time. There was no way she could deep throat his dick as she had done Fat Jerome's on numerous occasions. "Damn, Ericka, don't stop. Ssshit," he moaned. Ericka knew he was about to cum, because she felt his dick jumpin', coupled with him squeezing tight the hair on her head. So she sucked and tickled his balls at the same time. "Yes, Ericka, yesss, suck this thug dick, baby. Ahhh."

He released his thug juice all in her mouth. And like a true thug girl, she swallowed it like it was a liquid vitamin that was good for her health. She continued suckin' and lickin' his dick 'til he was rejuvenated and ready to fuck. She couldn't wait to accept his big dick. And he couldn't wait to deliver it. She lay back in the missionary position and allowed him to get on top of her. He placed his finger on her pussy lips and found she was wet as a muthafucka. He then put his dick on her pussy lips, ready to make a grand entry.

"Easy, big boy," Ericka said as she placed her hands on his waist to prevent him from thrusting his dick all the way up in her wet but tight pussy. He entered her about three inches.

She cocked her head back and inhaled through her teeth, simultaneously looking upward into his eyes. "Please, Osama, daddy, don't hurt it," she moaned. He moved his penis in her slowly, in and out, placing a little more dick up in her with every stroke.

"You like this dick, don't you?" said Osama.

"Yesss," she moaned, burying her nails deep into his back.

"Under any other circumstances I would make you pay for this dick," he said, working his dick strong and hard 'til he found her G-spot.

"It's worth it, I swear it is. Ahhh, yes, it isss. You fuckin' the hell out of me."

"You want me to stop?" he teased.

"No, please don't. I'm cummin'."

She wrapped her legs around his waist and let him have his way up in her, like her pussy belonged to him and only him. Before the night was out, he had caused her to experience four strong-ass orgasms. She made up her mind thereafter that anytime he wanted to fuck, her pussy would be available at his beckoning.

After fucking like rabbits all damn night just about, Osama and Ericka focused their attention on the real reason they were in Atlanta. They went back over to Veronda's crib. But again like last night, they received no answer. She wasn't home and she wasn't at all answering her phone. Ericka couldn't understand it. Just a few days ago, Veronda had called her and told her that she was contemplating strippin' again and that other than needing a little money, all was well in the ATL. Now days later she couldn't even get Veronda to answer her phone, let alone her door. Something had to be wrong, Ericka felt within. She just didn't know what. Osama didn't want to stay in the ATL another night with false hopes they would eventually catch her at home. Instead, he said to Ericka, "Fuck it!"

They then headed back to the Queen City. Osama elected not to call Fat Jerome about them not being able to reach Veronda at all. Osama knew that Fat Jerome would only want them to wait it out. Osama figured that if he waited it out, he and Ericka would be fuckin' up a storm and at the moment booty was not his number one priority. Business was. So he drove their asses back to Charlotte. Ericka sucked his dick damn near the whole way back, along with playing in her own pussy. Osama thought to himself that the bitch certainly had a fuckin' white liver, because her ass didn't get enough of sex! They call people with white livers oversexed.

They pulled up to Fat Jerome's house from the back side. When they circled around his big-ass house to park in the front they were greeted by some unexpected visitors.

"Get out of the car with your hands up!" It was the FBI, and they were all over the place.

Osama looked over at Ericka. "Bitch, I know you didn't set me up."

23

Let It Go, Capone

"Capone, baby, c'mere. You ain't gon' believe this shit."

"What is it now, Night-Night?" he said, walking out of the bathroom, drying his hair with a towel.

Night-Night pointed at the television. "Look at that shit," she said.

"It's just the fuckin' six o'clock news. You call me to watch the news, Night-Night?"

"Hell no! You know better than that. Whose face is that?"

"Where?"

"Hold on. They gon' show it again. Right there, right there."

"Oh, snap! How in the hell they get this bitch-ass nigga?" said Capone, as Fat Jerome's picture was being aired over the six o'clock news. "Wait, baby, let's see what the fuck this news lady saying." Both Capone and Night-Night listened intently while the anchorwoman spoke on the matter.

"FBI agents raided the home of one of Charlotte's most feared drug dealers. Agents say that Jeremiah Jerome Jenkins, aka Fat Jerome, is responsible for heading one of the most ruthless drug organizations they have ever investigated here in Mecklenburg County. Agents say that Jeremiah Jerome Jenkins's home had been bugged for some time now. They say that his home was also under constant surveillance, and that information gathered reveals that Jeremiah Jerome Jenkins ordered several murders, including a possible murder attempt that agents indicated may have been intercepted in another state.

"In the words of one of the leading FBI agents assigned to this case, 'It is a good day for law enforcement to have finally arrested Jeremiah Jerome Jenkins. We have been after him for a while now. However, thanks to some hard work and tips from others, three hundred kilos of cocaine were seized from Mr. Jenkins's home, along with five kilos of heroin and seven hundred thousand dollars in cash. Two other members of his gang have been arrested as well. And more arrests are sure to follow. Like I men-

tioned, this is a good day for law enforcement. It also is a good day for so many communities that want drugs out of the hands of their inhabitants. Mr. Jenkins and his crew were believed to be supplying most of the drugs on the north side of Charlotte. His gang is also responsible for a lot of the violence on the north side as well. We hope his arrest sends a big message to all the drug dealers and so-called gangs that law enforcement is working together and every branch and department will do everything in our power to see to it that our mission to clean up the drug-infested streets is accomplished.'

"Those were the words of FBI Agent Tom Stoakly. As I said, he was one of the leading FBI agents assigned to bring down Jeremiah Jerome Jenkins and his gang. No bond has been set for Mr. Jenkins or anyone arrested with him."

"Damn, them muthafuckas took a lot of shit from that fat-ass nigga," said Capone. "Shit, who in the hell would have believed that the nigga was keeping all of that coke, heroin, and cash at his crib, where he fuckin' lays his head?"

"That just goes to show you that muthafuckas out here ain't as smart as you may think they are," said Night-Night.

"Shit, I just wish we could have gotten to his ass before the feds did."

"Yeah, but, Capone, I'm certainly glad we pulled out when we did. Ain't no fuckin' tellin' what we would have gotten ourselves into fuckin' with this cat. I mean, baby, think about it. We catch the nigga in his crib slippin', blow his fuckin' brains all over the place only to later be apprehended by the feds? We just heard the damn anchorwoman on the news say that his crib was bugged and fuckin' heavily under surveillance."

"You right, baby girl. But fuck it, we ought to head over to the north side and rob every li'l cat selling drugs over there we see on a block. You know all of them niggas over that way work for Fat Jerome."

"Baby, fuck them. The feds are all over the place. It's hotter than the Fourth of July out there. Let's just chill and wait until the fire go out."

"Shit, Night-Night, all them niggas will be locked up by then."

"So fuckin what? Whatcha want, to get locked up too? Capone, the feds are everywhere."

"Yeah, but it's always somebody slippin'. Always. Now get your gun ready 'cause we 'bout to go on a mission."

"No, we are not, Capone. That's suicide."

"So you fuckin' punkin' out on me now?" Capone said, looking at Night-Night hard.

"You know fuckin' betta than to say some shit like that," replied Night-Night. "I'm your girl and I'm loyal all the way down to my toes, but I don't feel right about going over to the north side to jack them li'l niggas who work for Fat Jerome."

"Then stay here, Night-Night. I'll do it solo."

"Why can't you and I just go out to eat somewhere and just enjoy one another, Capone? Huh? Why can't we do that?"

"'Cause I don't like Fat Jerome and them niggas associated with him. They fuckin' killed my brother, Night-Night."

"Tye-Tye killed your brother, and Tye-Tye is dead. Fat Jerome just got picked up by the feds. When they finish with him he's gonna wish he was dead. The shit is over, baby."

"Look, Night-Night, the fact remains that the nigga ain't dead and some of his boys are still out here with major cash. I got—"

"Let it go, Capone. Please, baby, just let it gooo."

"Let it go? Let it go and fuckin' what, Night-Night?"

"And live to see another day, baby. That's all I'm saying. Damn!"

Capone walked over to the bed in the hotel room. He lifted the mattress and retrieved his

.357 Magnum. Night-Night looked on as he did so. He checked it for bullets. It was fully loaded. He placed it at his waist, down his pants, and pulled his shirt over it. Capone then looked over at Night-Night. "You rollin' wit' me or not?"

"Capone, baby, please don't do this to me, to us."

"Don't do what, Night-Night? Try to put more money in our pocket so that we can live betta later on?"

"It ain't about the money, Capone."

"What the fuck is it about then?"

Night-Night stood up in his face. "Thinkin', Capone. It's about thinkin'. I keep tellin' you now ain't the time. Why do you insist that it is?"

"I told you that I don't like none of them muthafuckas. They need to fuckin' feel my wrath. They need to fuckin' know that they picked the wrong nigga's brother to kill."

"It's not gonna bring your brother back, baby. Listen to me. You just got out a few months ago. The only thing that was on your mind was getting revenge for your brother's death. Okay, we got that. Now, you want more. You want riches. Money'll come later, baby."

"How much later? You know how much money we got? We only have like thirteen thousand."

"Don't matter. We'll figure something out. We always do. What matters right now at this very moment is that you and I have each other. You said it for yourself that you missed the hell out of me when you had to be away for three years. Shit, baby, you think I didn't missed the fuck out of you? I missed you every single day. Now that you're here and your brother's killer is six feet deep thanks to me putting two fuckin' bullets in his head, let's move on and just enjoy one another. Can we do that, baby? Can we just please do that?"

"Night-Night—"

"No, baby, just simply answer my question," she said, cutting him off.

"Okay, you got that. But—"

Again she cut him off. "No 'buts,' Capone," she said, placing her lips on his to kiss. "I love you so muchhhh," she said. "Let's just chill." She unbuttoned his shirt and removed his gun. She placed his gun back underneath the mattress, unbuckled his belt, eased his jeans down along with his underwear, and started blessing his jimmy with her tongue and mouth. She knew that if nothing else would change his mind momentarily, giving him a good dick suckin' would.

***

"Derrick, c'mere a minute," his mother yelled. It was 11:43 p.m. and his mother had just gotten in from work. She was in the kitchen, pouring orange juice to take with her meds.

"Yes, ma'am?" he said as he walked into the kitchen.

"Mike-Mike called me earlier and told me that you had picked him up from school again today. I noticed you've been spending a lot of time with him since you've been out. Even saw you yesterday helping him with his homework. Prison must've really done you some good, boy."

Derrick smiled at what his mother said. "I just wanna see Mike-Mike being the best he can be, that's all."

"Well, he's got a head on his shoulders, that's for sure. The boy can read far better than I will ever be able to."

"He's definitely sharp as a knife. I'ma stay on him every chance I get, too."

"So did you find you a job?"

"I'm still looking. I went and enrolled in barber college the day before yesterday though. I should be hearing something by next week. In the meantime, Momma, I'm thinking hard about maybe creating my own business. Nothing big though."

"Whatchu got in mind, Derrick?"

"Selling name brand tennis shoes and clothing. I saw a guy yesterday at the car wash off of West Trade Street selling nice shoes and clothing out of his van. He told me that he travels to New York at least once a month and buys shoes and clothing real cheap then brings 'em back down here and sells them for a nice profit."

"Yeah, but you would need a small business license."

"I know, Momma. He schooled me on all of that."

"You will also need cash. I assume you're gonna wait until you get yourself a job before you try going into business for yourself?"

Derrick thought before he spoke, and then said, "Momma, I love you. And I am not gonna lie to you ever again like I used to prior to me having to leave to go away to prison. So I'ma be straight with you and let you know that I have a few dollars, and I—"

His mother cut him off and looked at him strangely. "Whatchu mean, you have a few dollars? Where did you get these few dollars from?"

"When I was doing wrong, I was saving my money, Momma. I got a nice li'l penny."

"So, you telling me that you still got dirty money?"

"Momma, money is money."

"Don't get smart with me, Derrick. Just answer my question. You still got dirty money?"

"Yes, ma'am, I do," Derrick truthfully answered.

"Where is it?" his mother asked.

"Hold on a moment, Momma," Derrick said. He then went into his room and came back.

His mother saw him carrying a black book bag. He laid the bag on the glass kitchen dinner table, opened it up, and dumped nothing but stacks of cash out onto the table. The sight of all that cash stunned his mother. "Derrick, are you sure you're not selling them drugs again? Don't lie to me."

"Momma, I swear on the grave of my father that I'm not selling that stuff anymore."

"Well, how much money is this, Derrick?"

"Almost seventeen."

"Seventeen thousand?"

"Yes, ma'am. And, Momma, please don't think that I'm back hustling. I'm through with that. I'm not lying to you."

"That money is still dirty, Derrick."

"Momma, no disrespect, but it's not the money, it's the mind behind the money. My mind is clear now. I just want you to have whatever you want out of this cash and to start me a small business with the rest. That's all I want."

Derrick's mother walked away from the sight of all the cash on the table. She went to the sink and began rinsing out the glass that she had orange juice in. She shook her head from left to right. "I can't accept dirty money, Derrick."

"Please, Momma, take at least five grand. Please, just do that for me and spend it on whatever you like."

"I can't accept it," she turned around and replied facing him. "The Bible says, 'What would it profit a man to gain the world and lose his soul?' Like I said, that money is dirty. You gained it through capitalizing off of someone else's weakness."

Derrick looked at his mother with a confused expression on his face. "I don't understand, Momma. What you mean, I gained this money through capitalizing off of someone else's weakness?"

"Using drugs is a weakness that many find hard to say no to. When you capitalize off of that, Derrick, you are no better than the person on the drugs. People on drugs need help. They don't need somebody's hand pushing them more drugs."

"Momma, people have their own choice. It ain't like I ever put a gun to someone's head and demanded that they buy drugs from me."

"You don't have to, Derrick. Their weakness is the gun that demands them to go out and get the drugs. But if the drug user doesn't have anyone to buy his drugs from then guess what? That person would be forced to quit. Simply put, I can't and won't have anything to do with drug money. If you want to use it for whatever you have planned, then suit yourself. But knowing exactly where that money there came from, I can't accept it."

Derrick didn't say anything further on the matter. His mother was solid in her stance as she had always been when it came down to this type of stuff. Derrick didn't want to offend her in any way by trying to persuade her otherwise. At this moment in her life, healing from breast cancer, he just wanted her to be at peace. He put the money back into the book bag and was about to go to his room. His mother stopped him though before he got the chance. "Come over here before you go back in there," she said in a very gentle, sweet voice.

Derrick stood directly in front of her with his book bag full of cash hanging over one of his shoulders. His mother reached out and started caressing his right cheek with the open palm of her hand. She looked him deep in the eyes.

"I know that you can't change the wrong actions you committed yesterday. That's your past. You can only work hard today to ensure that you never repeat those wrong actions regardless of the circumstances. Now, next to being a Christian woman, let me tell you why I have never consciously received drug money from your hands. When I got that call years ago that your father had been found in an alley with a needle in his arm, and had died from a heroin overdose, I wondered, *who sold my husband that bag of dope that ended his life? How much did it cost?* Perhaps, Derrick, all the guy wanted who sold your father and my husband that bag of dope was another dollar. But you know what, son? That dollar, regardless of how much it was, had death on it.

"For a long time, I hated drug dealers with a passion. When I would ride to work and see them on the corner I would purposely get on my telephone and call the police. I wanted them all off the streets. I had even gotten me a gun once and was contemplating finding out who that guy was who sold your father dope. I wanted to just walk up to him and pull that trigger."

"You serious, Momma?"

"You ever known me to lie to you?"

"No, ma'am."

"All right then. I was as serious as serious can get. You just didn't know about it because you were a kid. Seven or eight years old, I believe."

"What stopped you?" Derrick curiously asked.

"God. God and the fact that I had you and Mike-Mike to still look after. God showed me that vengeance is His. And that I had to think and live for my kids. You and Mike-Mike had already lost your father. And had I killed somebody, y'all would have lost me, because I probably would have been on death row or in prison somewhere with a natural life sentence. Then you and Mike-Mike would have had to be raised up in a foster home somewhere."

"I'm so glad you let God help you change your mind. You are the best mother in the world. I used to think that you were mean and stuck in your ways. But, Momma, when I was in prison, I realized how much you just wanted me to do the right thing. You wanted me to be patient and to not make bad decisions. Above all, Momma, I realized that you had to be my mother and my father. I know that it wasn't easy. Because I had my mind fixed on doing things my way so many times. You are the only woman who visited me while I was in prison. You're the only woman who sent me money, cards, and letters. And you are the only woman who has always told me the truth, regardless of how I take it. I realize that you have done these things and soooo much more because you really love me. And, Momma, I love you for that. I love you for just being and staying you. There's no way I could ever repay you for who and what you are to me. But just know that you are appreciated."

"I know you appreciate me, Derrick. And I know you love me. But do me a favor."

"Anything, Momma. What?"

"Just never offer me drug money, 'cause I'm never gonna take it. I know you mean well, but—"

"I gotcha, Momma. I promise to never do that again. Truth is, I'm never gonna even sell drugs again."

"Oh, yeah, that's what I wanted to ask you. Tell me, what changed your mind about hustling drugs? I mean, I'm glad you did. But, Derrick, what brought you to that point? I'm curious."

Derrick thought immediately about Mike-Mike and the bad example he set for him prior to going to prison. Nothing in this world had hurt Derrick like finding out that his little brother had started hustling coke on the corner. Just thinking of Mike-Mike doing so was enough to bring Derrick to tears. He held them back though, and replied, "I just wanna be a good example for my little brother and not end up dead in the streets or back in prison."

"But isn't that what I have been trying to get across to you for so long?"

"Yeah, but sometimes, Momma, some of us have to learn the hard way. Things have to happen in our lives for us to see the light and come to our senses."

"What about that girl you were dating? How is she?" his mother asked, while putting her glass onto the kitchen counter and then slowly walking out. Derrick followed her into the living room.

"I haven't heard from Veronda in a long while, Momma."

"Well, what's a long while?"

"Two years," he replied.

"You saying that you didn't hear from her at all while you were incarcerated, Derrick?"

"I'm saying that, and I'm saying that women are a trip."

Derrick's mother gave him a look that read, "Wait a minute, 'cause I'm a woman too."

Derrick caught on quick to his mother's facial expression. "Let me explain, Momma, before you slap me, because that's exactly what you look like you were about to do when I said that."

His mother put her hand on her hip and poked her lips outward. "Ummm, hmmm, I sho' was," she said.

Derrick smiled. "Momma, you ain't changed a bit. But what I meant was one minute a woman will tell you that she loves you, then the next she'll turn around and treat you as if those three words never escaped her lips. Before I caught that gun charge, Momma, Veronda had decided that it would be best if she moved out of Charlotte."

"But why, Derrick?"

"Well, she got caught up in a situation that had interfered with her comfort zone. I'll say it like that. I didn't want her to go, Momma. I swear I didn't because I had deep feelings for her, but she insisted that leaving would be the best thing for her. Despite me trying to convince her otherwise, she kissed me good-bye."

"Just like that, huh?"

"Well, she promised that within six months of her settling into Atlanta that she would get in touch with me. She promised me that she would do this, Momma."

"Okay, but you ended up going to jail."

"Doesn't matter. She had our address."

"I can't dispute that, but, Derrick, listen. Veronda is just one woman. You're young, and handsome, baby. You know what that means?"

"What that mean, Momma?"

"That means you're gonna meet a lot of women before you die, God willing. Some of them you're not gonna like at all. Others you will swear that heaven has come down to greet you, trust me. These are the types of women who are gonna talk that talk you men like, and walk that walk. They look good, smell good, dress good, all that. But that doesn't mean that they are all good. Most of the women you're gonna meet will be no more than eye candy. Something that's designed to cause you to lust. And trust me, Derrick, sometimes lust feels just like love. But I assure you, there's a difference."

"What's the difference, Momma?" Derrick curiously asked.

"I'ma answer that, then I'm going to bed. I've been on my feet all day and I'm tired. Now listen to me. One word can help you know the difference between love and lust. That word is patience. When you lust for something, you want it right then. Everything inside you is saying, 'I got to have that!' But when you love someone, you are forced to be patient because love doesn't work, Derrick, outside of its developmental stage. Let me just say it like this: Love is like a woman who has just conceived. The woman knows she is with child, but she can't enjoy the beauty of that child until the proper time. The proper time, Derrick, is after the growth and development stage. When that time is up, the woman carrying the child's water breaks. This lets her know that the time to bring forth her child has come. But until that breaking point, she had to remain patient.

"Now, I don't know a lot about your girl-friend, Veronda. I just know that the two of y'all were together a whole lot, and every time I looked around you were on that cell phone of yours, talking to her. Plus, your room was decorated with a blown-up picture of her. Witnessing all that kinda let me know that the two of you were feeling each other. You say that she left you, but promised to write, yet didn't. Well, you're home now. If the two of you were really meant to be together and really had love for each other, then guess what? That love will allow y'all to reconnect, somehow, someway. You just got to be patient. My mother, your grandmother, used to tell me when I was young, 'If you love someone and you let them go and they come back to you then it was meant to be.' You just got to be patient, Derrick, and wait on the breaking point. That's if love was between you and Veronda and not just lust. Now, I'm going to bed."

Derrick kissed his mother good night. "Momma, I love you." He then went to his room and thought hard on everything that she had shared with him. But before he settled down for the night, he peeped into Mike-Mike's room and saw that Mike-Mike had fallen asleep with a book laid over his chest. It was the autobiography of Thurgood Marshall. Mike-Mike was sleeping so soundly and peacefully that Derrick didn't bother to remove the book from his chest. Instead, he hit the light switch on the wall, cutting the light out, and eased back into his room for bed.

24

Ignorance Is A Cure For Nothing!

"So, what you know about Thurgood Marshall, Mike-Mike? I saw you with his book on your chest and whatnot last night," said Derrick as he drove Mike-Mike to school.

"Yeah, I was tired, bruh. I've been studying real hard lately. But, umm, Thurgood Marshall, he's a remarkable guy. I didn't know it until I read his book. He was the first African American to be appointed to the Supreme Court of the United States."

"Who appointed him?" asked Derrick. He just wanted to see primarily just how much information his little brother had actually taken in from reading about this historic African American.

"Lyndon B. Johnson appointed him," Mike-Mike replied with no hesitation.

"Okay. You right. Now how long did he serve on the Supreme Court?"

Mike-Mike thought a second or two. "Ummm, he served from 1967 to 1991."

"Dammmmmn, knucklehead! You got a photographic memory, huh?"

Mike-Mike cracked a smile. "Li'l somethin' somethin'," he replied.

"That's good though, 'cause hell, you know what they say right?"

"What's that, bruh?"

"They say if you ever want to hide something from a black man, put it in a book."

"Why they say that?" asked Mike-Mike.

"Because they know that very few of us take the time to read. I used to read all the time before I got sidetracked selling drugs and whatnot. But while in prison I started back reading. Knowledge is power."

"I know," Mike-Mike agreed.

"I was reading up on W.E.B. Du Bois. You know what he said, Mike-Mike?"

"What's that?"

"He said, 'Ignorance is a cure for nothing!' That statement stayed with me. It stayed with me because I began looking back over how stupid I was to not have taken my time and just let what's gon' be, be. What I mean by that, li'l bruh, is this: I didn't have to sell drugs in an effort to get us out the hood. I knew better. See that's what ignorance is: it's when you know better, but refuse to do better. I had refused to do better because I had started figuring in my own mind that if I sold drugs and made this or that amount of money fast, I could perhaps save enough to accomplish my goal. But in the streets and being a part of that dope game, things don't always go as you plan them. They never will. Me selling drugs led to me carrying a gun. And carrying a gun led to me ending up in prison."

"Not to cut you off, bruh, but Momma told me that the judge had given you sixty months, and that you would have to do eighty-five percent of that prison sentence."

"Momma was right," said Derrick as he pulled up at Mike-Mike's school.

"Then how is it you're home after only doing a year and a half? Did they cut your time for taking classes? 'Cause I remember you writing and telling me that you were taking a vocational training course of some sort."

"I was."

"So that's how you got out of prison early then, huh?"

Derrick looked at Mike-Mike. He reached and rubbed his hand over and across Mike-Mike's head. "You're full of questions just like I used to be when I was your age," Derrick said.

"I'm just curious, that's all," replied Mike-Mike.

"Don't be. Some things, Mike-Mike, are best left unsaid."

"Oh, like the time your girlfriend made me feel good, and you told me to never ever tell Momma about it."

"Exactly. Did you ever tell her? Tell me the truth now."

Mike-Mike looked at Derrick with his lips poked outward. "Bruh, I gave you my word that I wouldn't ever say anything about that. And I haven't. There's no way I could ever rat you out. I love you."

"You love me, huh?"

"Derrick, bruh, I love you to death. It literally killed me inside when you left to go to prison. I ain't gon' lie, I couldn't study right or nothing. I just lost my drive, bruh."

"Well, are you focused now that I am here?"

"I'm focused like never before and I'm happy. It's hard to be happy when you're not focused. And when you're not focused you can't get anything done right," said Mike-Mike.

"That's a very true statement. But now that you are focused, are you gonna continue to do the right thing?"

"I don't have a choice."

"You always got a choice, Mike-Mike."

"Not as long as you're home, I don't."

"Boy, get out of my car," said Derrick, pushing Mike-Mike against the passenger's side door.

"I'm just keeping it real, bruh. You ain't gon' let me do anything wrong."

"Yeah, but I can't watch you twenty-four/seven, Mike-Mike."

"For real for real, bruh, you don't even have to. Like I said, I got my focus back, and I'm just happy that my big brother's home. Now, I gotta go 'cause I hear our school bell ringing; that means it's almost time for class to start."

"A'ight then. I love you," said Derrick

"Love you too, bruh."

Capone pulled his Cadillac Escalade into the driveway of Night-Night's parents' home.

"Night-Night, you know how much I hate coming over here to your mother and father's house. Your mother fuckin' hates my guts and you know that."

"So what? Now are you coming in or not, Capone?"

"Honestly, I prefer not to. And I really wish you wouldn't try to persuade me differently."

Night-Night inhaled and exhaled hard. "You know how fuckin' nosy my damn parents' neighbors are. Shit, if they see you sitting out here in the driveway with your baseball cap turned backward and your stunna shades on, coupled with your ride being a damn all-black chromed-out Cadillac Escalade, it ain't gon' do nothing but give them something to wonder and talk about. They already talking about not seeing me in church the last couple of weeks."

"Fuck 'em, Night-Night, let 'em talk. Shit, that's what nosy-ass neighbors do."

Night-Night sucked her teeth. "Just come on in with me, Capone. Hell, I ain't gon' be but a few minutes. I just gotta grab a few things."

"I'ma come, but, Night-Night, I'm telling you don't take fuckin' forever up in there. I know how your mother is; she'll start looking at me all crazy and shit, and I don't like that."

"Just don't pay her any attention, Capone, baby. Just don't pay her any attention."

Capone grabbed his .357 Magnum from underneath his seat and stuck it down his pants.

Night-Night looked on and shook her head. "That's not even necessary, Capone," she said.

"Shit, it is for me," he replied.

Night-Night rolled her eyes. "Whatever," she shot back, before the both of them headed inside her parents' home.

***

"So how much money you thinking about investing, Derrick?" asked Abdullah. Abdullah was a Muslim who sold clothes and shoes from his van. Derrick had been talking to him off and on since he been out of prison about starting a small business.

"I don't know. Maybe five or six grand. Would that be enough for me to get a good jumpstart?" Derrick replied.

"Five grand is good. But if you had ten, I would allow you to go into business with me. I'll sell all our items," Abdullah assured him.

"Hold up, Abdullah. You telling me that if I just straight out gave you ten Gs all I would have to do is let you handle everything and all I would have to do is chill and collect profit?"

"That's exactly what I'm saying."

"I wouldn't have to go downtown to get a business license or nothing?"

"Derrick, I already got all of that. Now, look, I'm going to New York tomorrow. I got a lot of shit lined up for me already. My people there got Gucci, Prada, Sean John, Baby Phat, Apple Bottoms gear, Air Force Ones, Jordans, all of that."

"Damn, Abdullah, that's what's up, man. So, investing ten Gs will earn me how much of a profit?"

"About five," Abdullah replied without hesitation.

"Five Gs?" Derrick incredulously asked. *Damn, this shit too good to be true.*

"Five thousand, yep," Abdullah said, snapping Derrick out of his brief contemplation.

"Well, I tell you what—"

"Hold on a minute Derrick," Abdullah said, cutting Derrick off only to step to the side with a guy who had motioned for his attention. Derrick saw Abdullah and the guy get into Abdullah's van. Derrick used the moment alone to think about making the $10,000 investment.

Inside the van, however, a transaction was being made. The guy handed Abdullah a sandwich bag.

"What I owe you for this?" asked Abdullah, looking at the bag that was handed to him and opening it.

The guy looked at Abdullah. "First of all, that's some raw shit. It'll make your nose bleed, no bullshit."

"Just tell me how much, man," Abdullah replied.

"That's half an ounce. Fourteen grams. Make it a thousand."

"A thousand for fourteen grams?"

"Naw. That's five hundred. You owe me five hundred for the last one I gave you. And I'm telling you, Abdullah, I need my money, man."

"I got you. Just trust me on that. Matta fact, I'ma have it tomorrow."

"Don't play with me, now. Have my fuckin' money, man. This shit don't grow on trees," the guy said, before exiting Abdullah's van. Abdullah stuck the sandwich bag into his pocket, and then called Derrick over to his van.

"So, Derrick, you gon' invest or not? Like I said, I'm heading to New York tomorrow."

"How soon today can I get you the money?" asked Derrick.

"You can get it to me as soon as possible. I'll be right here for another hour or two." Just like Derrick, Abdullah saw an opportunity that he wasn't gonna let slip away. Abdullah was sick. But Derrick couldn't see it.

"Good. I'll be back shortly," Derrick said, and then headed to his mother's crib to retrieve the cash.

Night-Night's father greeted her when she walked into the living room of her parents' home with Capone. "Heyyyy, baby girl. I was wondering when you were gonna show up. Haven't seen you in what, a hundred years?"

"It's only been three weeks, Daddy," replied Night-Night, kissing her father on his left cheek. "Daddy, you've met Capone, my fiancé."

"Fiancé? Boy, you planning on making my daughter yo' wife?" he said, reaching his hand out to shake Capone's hand.

"If she says so, sir. She's the boss."

"She's the boss?" Night-Night's father repeated. "Hell, I see why y'all gon' get married. Both of y'all crazy. Now crazy plus crazy equals what? Double crazy! Simple mathematics." Night-Night and Capone laughed. "Oh, y'all think it's funny, but people gon' have something on their hands dealing with two crazy folks."

"Daddy, ain't nothing crazy about either of us," Night-Night said, smiling.

"Be damned if it ain't. The man said that you was the boss. Now, anybody crazy enough to let you be their boss, that person can't be the sharpest knife in the kitchen."

Capone didn't crack a smile at that joke. It offended his intelligence and Night-Night felt it. She, therefore, took hold of Capone's arms gently and kissed him. She then said, "Daddy, crazy or not, we love each other and that's all that matters."

"I know y'all do. But, hell, baby girl, what does love have to do with it? You heard what Tina Turner said."

"Love has everything to do with it," Night-Night shot back.

"Baby girl, take it from me. Love is blind. I called myself loving your mother when the two of us were in our late teens. Guess what?"

"What, Daddy?"

"Now I'm stuck with her big ass for the rest of my life," he joked.

"Daddy, stop it," Night-Night said, laughing. Even Capone cracked a smile.

"Your mother don't wanna exercise, or nothing. She and that lady Madea could pass for twins. All your mother wants to do is cook, of course, clean, go to church, and read her Bible. I ain't kidding, baby girl. She's upstairs right now, in the room, sitting in her favorite recliner, reading that Bible of hers."

"She is, Daddy?" asked Night-Night.

"Why you think I spend the majority of my time downstairs? All your mother does is call me the devil. Would the devil build his wife a home from the damn ground up? This is her heaven right here. Now would the devil build something this damn beautiful for her? Would the devil even buy her a Mercedes for her to ride all over the city in and to church? All the women at her church are jealous as hell of her. Including the preacher's wife. They wish they had some of the things your mother's got."

"I know, Daddy," said Night-Night. "I know."

"Not just that. Some of them women down there at that church be winking their eye at me and everything. They do it, because they want what your momma got. Then she got the nerve to ask me why I don't like going to church with her like I used to. When I told her what some of them ladies down at that church be doing to me, guess what she had the nerve to say, baby girl?"

"What, Daddy?"

"She had the nerve to say that I must have been doing something to entice them women to wink their eye at me and lift their dress to reveal their thighs."

"She accused you of being in the wrong, Daddy?"

"I told you, she calls me the devil. The other day I went to use the toilet. I mistakenly urinated a little on the toilet seat and forgot to wipe it off. When your mother went in there and came out all I could hear her say was, 'Devil, I rebuke you.' Then she said, 'Next time, wipe it off!' That's why that love thing you talking about, trust me, a whole lot comes with that."

"Fredrick, who that down there you talkin' to?" Night-Night's mother yelled.

"Bring ya big butt down here and see," Night-Night's father replied.

"Devil, I rebuke you," she snapped while making her way down the stairway. She saw Night-Night and Capone next to each other, sitting on the sofa. Her greeting was not as warm as Night-Night's father's, as she looked at Night-Night. "Oh, you must need some money." She then gave Capone the evil eye and walked into the kitchen.

It took Derrick no time at all to retrieve the ten Gs. He did so in such a hurry that one would have thought someone put a gun to his head and threatened him to do so. All he could seem to think about while retrieving the cash was the profit that Abdullah told him that he would eventually receive if he decided to make the investment. Derrick felt good about making this move. He had seen how people flocked to Abdullah's van to purchase the product that he had to offer them at a price that they could afford. From the look of it, Abdullah had a damn good thing going. Becoming partners with him was an opportunity that Derrick felt he could not pass up by any means. He, therefore, delivered the cash to Abdullah.

"That's ten stacks," Derrick said, as he and Abdullah sat in Abdullah's van.

"You sure it's all there?" replied Abdullah. "'Cause this business now."

"I put it on my life, it's all there," Derrick assured him. Abdullah sniffled as if he had a cold. He kept doing it and running his finger underneath his nose as he put Derrick's ten Gs in his glove compartment.

"Sounds like you coming down with a cold, Abdullah," Derrick said.

Abdullah sniffled again with his finger underneath his nose. "I just got bad allergies that's all," Abdullah replied. "I've had allergies all my life," he lied. Truth is, Abdullah was on drugs, heavy. Derrick couldn't see it, because Abdullah didn't look the part of a drug addict. He was healthy looking and clean with nice clothes. However, unbeknownst to Derrick, the ten Gs was not a business move, but a bailout for the shyster.

Night-Night followed her mother into the kitchen. "Momma, you just gon' come down stairs and not even say hi?" asked Night-Night.

"Why should I? I'm your mother and you haven't been over here to check on your father and me in what, a month?"

"Three weeks, Momma. That's all it's been. I've been a little busy that's all."

"Busy doing what? Fooling around with that boy out there? I see he's out of prison."

"He's been out a few months," said Night-Night.

"Yeah, and he's probably up to no good."

"Momma, how could you say that? He's my fiancé and I love him very much."

"How can I say that? I can say that because my spirit don't steer me wrong."

"Your spirit?" asked Night-Night.

"Yes, my spirit. The spirit that God gave me to discern when something isn't right."

"Momma, what about my heart? What about how I feel?"

"What about it?" her mother snapped. "I even dreamed about you a few nights ago. You know what I dreamed? I dreamed that you walked into this house with a monkey on your back."

"A monkey?" Night-Night asked.

"Yeah, a monkey. It was on your back. You were trying to get it off, but it had such a grip around your head that you couldn't plow him loose. When I awoke from that dream, I got down on my knees and prayed, 'Lord Jesus, I don't know what my daughter is going through, but, Lord, please don't let the monkey destroy her.'"

Tears started welling up in Night-Night's eyes. She fought them though. Her mother continued right on talking, despite Night-Night's hurt.

"Do you know what it means when you see a monkey in your dream? It means that the devil is present."

"So, what you saying, Momma, that I'm demon possessed or something?"

"All I'm saying is something's wrong. I didn't have that dream for nothing. Not just that, but when was the last time you had a job? I know. You can't remember. And that's a shame. Your father and I worked hard to put you through college. You got a degree in accounting and won't even use it. Instead, you come over here and expect your father and me to continue to support you?"

"Momma, you and Daddy don't have to do nothing for me."

"Not since your drug-dealing boyfriend been out," her mother hissed.

"He doesn't sell drugs anymore, Momma, for one. Second—"

"Girl, please. That boy got the streets written all over him."

"Momma, please, let's just not go—"

"No. We are going there," her mother said, cutting her off. "We're going there because you're wasting your life with a thug who can't love you."

"He does love me, Momma. You can't read another person's heart."

"Then why are the two of you staying in a hotel? That's exactly where you called me from a few weeks ago, because I traced the call. That's one thing I can say about your father: he has never taken me to any hotel to lay up with me. He told me once that if he couldn't sleep with me in a bed that he paid for in a house of our own, he wouldn't sleep with me at all. Now unless you have found you a man who resembles your father, then trust me, you haven't found you a man at all."

"So, son, be perfectly honest with me if you don't mind," Night-Night's father said to Capone as they both sat in the living room. "Do you really love my daughter? Or are the two of you just caught up in lust for one another?"

Capone smiled after hearing the question. He then replied, "I love the hell out of your daughter, sir. And that's as real as it gets."

"Yeah, but, son, didn't you just do like three years in the joint?"

"Yes, I did. And your daughter stuck by me the whole time. Visited me every week and everything. In fact, had I not gone to the joint I never would have known just how much I'm really in love with her."

"You had to go to the joint to discover that?" Night-Night's father asked.

Capone thought before he spoke. He was in the presence of an elderly man who had gray all in his head. To Capone, this symbolized wisdom. He knew that this elderly man of wisdom loved his daughter, Night-Night. So, with every question concerning the two of them as a couple, Capone didn't want to look stupid. But he wanted to at least attempt to give an answer of substance.

Meanwhile, Night-Night and her mother were at it, uncompromisingly.

"Momma, there are a lot of things that you don't know about Calvin. But I know that he is a good man and I'm not gonna stop loving him for no one. Besides, you didn't let nothing stop you from marrying Daddy," Night-Night said, as she and her mother continued their discourse in the kitchen.

"Your father had enough sense and courage to change."

"What? You don't think Calvin can change? Momma, nothing happens overnight. You, being in the church and all, should know this."

"Girl, don't get smart with me now, ya hear? You watch how you talk to me in my house."

"I'm not trying to get smart or anything with you."

"Ya betta not be, because I'm yo' momma, and, girl, I will put the fear of God in you so quick up in this kitchen that it would take the Lord Jesus Christ to come from His home in glory to get me up off of ya. You hear me?"

Night-Night felt herself getting highly upset. She felt that her mother was so self-righteous and so into seeing things her way that she couldn't see someone else's point of view. She thought momentarily how all while she was growing up, her mother wanted her to be this kind of girl and that kind of girl. She was so tired of being up under her mother's control that she vowed that once she got old enough to do what she wanted to do, that would be exactly what she did.

She snapped out of briefly thinking and reflecting on that when she heard her mother say, "And for your information, when your father was selling heroin years ago, I brutally contested what he was doing."

"Yeah, but you still loved him, Momma, and refused to leave him."

"Yes, I loved your father. But make no mistake about it, I was gonna leave him."

"Then why didn't you, Momma? Tell me that? Why you just didn't leave him and find you some college graduate on his way to being a doctor or a lawyer or something? Someone who didn't have a street background and whatnot?"

"Because your father had gotten robbed and shot. He had to be in a wheelchair and he needed me. How could I walk away from him at such a tragic time in his life? I couldn't."

"Neither can I just walk away from my man, Momma. He's not perfect. Like all human beings he has made a lot of mistakes. But we love each other and he really needs me in his life, just like Dad needed you."

"Tell me, what does this thug of a guy need from you? You don't have a job, because you quit. You haven't given him any babies, thank God. You are rebellious as they come. Won't listen to me or your father, so what makes you think you are gonna listen to your husband when you do get one? You are definitely unladylike, because what kind of a woman who is not from the streets would allow somebody who is from the streets to not only have her without responsibility, but change her for the worse in the process? Now, you got on ya li'l makeup. And the clothes you got on make you look nice as well. But, you are my daughter. I carried you for nine months straight. Your father and I raised you. I know ya up and down. And the woman I am beholding right now is definitely my daughter, but one I certainly did not raise to be as she is today."

"Well, however you see me, Momma, I just came over to check on you and Dad and to grab a few of my belongings. Not to argue, fuss, or fight. I know I got my issues. Certainly, I am not Holy Mother Mary. I am woman enough to admit that. I am also woman enough to know that if it weren't for the grace of God, you would not even be where you are right now. So, please, don't judge me. Only God can do that. That's why I stopped going to that church. Because all those women do there is talk about this and talk about that. The last time I was at your church, one of the ladies there was gossiping about the dress I wore. I heard the lady say to another, 'She know she ain't got no business wearing a dress that tight to church.' Another old lady was talking about my hair. I heard her say, 'She sho' got her hair done all up like how them worldly girls do their hair. Wonder who she trying to entice?' I am so tired of others trying to get me to be who they want me to be and whatnot. I am my own woman. I'm grown. If I want to go to hell with gasoline panties on, it's my choice. No one has the right to take my choice away from me, Momma. No one."

"Get your things and get out of my house. You, that thug boyfriend of yours, and the devil you got inside you," her mother snapped, pointing her finger toward the kitchen exit.

"I know it sounds crazy, but that's the way it was for me. I mean don't get me wrong, I was crazy about your daughter prior to me going to the joint. She was my girl. But I wasn't sure of her loyalty," Capone finally answered.

"You wasn't sure of her loyalty? I don't get that. Talk to me."

"What I mean is," replied Capone, "I wasn't sure if she could take me having to be gone for three years on a drug charge without her going on with her life and all. See, Pops, I come from the streets. The streets are all I know. My brother and I were adopted. We never knew our biological parents. Our adopted father used to drink real heavy. Whenever he was drunk, he would beat on me and my brother. Our adopted mother used to let him do it because she was afraid of him. Finally, when I was sixteen and my brother was fifteen, we left."

"Just like that? Without saying a word? Just up and left home?"

"Well, really it was more to it than us just up and leaving. Like I said, our adopted father was an alcoholic. One night he had gotten so drunk that he beat the shit out of my brother for simply not being able to find a necktie that our adopted father had misplaced. I was in my bedroom at the time, about to prepare for bed, when I heard my brother crying and screaming. He then came running into my bedroom with his shirt off. His back was whipped up and bleeding. A friend of mine had given me a .22 revolver a few weeks earlier. I had the gun hidden underneath my mattress. When I saw how badly my little brother was whipped up and bleeding from what our adopted father had done to him, I was furious. I grabbed my gun and went straight into the living room where he was and pointed my gun directly in his face. 'Why the fuck you beat on my brother like you did, muthafucka?'"

Night-Night's father interrupted Capone. "Try not to curse."

"Excuse me, I apologize for that," replied Capone.

"Personally, I don't care, but my wife, she's a devoted Christian. She doesn't even allow me to curse in this house."

"I understand, sir," Capone said.

"Okay, well, what happened when you pointed the gun in your adopted father's face?" inquired Night-Night's father.

"I told him tonight was the night that he was gonna meet his Maker. I was as serious as a heart attack. He looked up at me and said in a slurred voice, 'Boy, you betta get that gun away from my face.' I ain't doing nothing. Matter of fact, you betta start praying, 'cause you're a dead MF.' That's when my adopted mother came in. She was shocked to see me pointing a gun in her husband's face. Truth is, she didn't even know I had a gun nor the heart and nerve to have the barrel of it aimed right between her husband's eyes.

"'Calvin, put that gun away,' she said, trembling with her hands at her mouth. 'No,' I shouted. 'I'm tired of this sorry MF putting his hands on me and my brother. Enough is enough.' When I said that, Pops, my adopted father, reached for the gun, but he was so drunk that it made him too slow. I started beating him over the head with it. Blood started coming from his head. I just lost it. My adopted mother was screaming, 'Stop! Stop! You're gonna kill him, Calvin.'

"'That's exactly what I wanna do. I hate this MF!' I replied. I knew that I would have killed him that night if it weren't for my little brother. He came in the living room and pulled me off our adopted father. 'That's enough,' I heard my brother say. 'Man, that's enough. Let's just leave and never come back,' he said further. And, Pops, that's exactly what he and I did."

"Where did y'all go?"

"We went to a friend's house that night. Then we just started staying here and there until we started making money in the streets, selling drugs."

"So that's what you went to prison for? Selling drugs, right?"

"Right."

"Did your brother go too?"

"Noooo. But, Pops, I wish he would have," said Capone. His eyes began to water.

"Why you say that, son?"

"Because had he been in prison somewhere, he probably would be still alive. My brother was found with his throat cut from one end to the other."

"Oh my God. Who in the world would do such a thing?"

"He was in and out of the streets. Those things happen. I just wish it would've happened to someone else."

"Well, I'm sorry to hear that, son, about your brother."

"Like I said, those things happen in the streets. But back to your daughter. I love her more than words could ever allow me to express. I want her to be my wife one day. Because, like I said, she could have gone on with her life once I went to the joint, but she didn't. Not just that though, Pops. Your daughter isn't from the streets. I didn't meet her there. I met her at a homecoming football game at Johnson C. Smith University. I was there with a partner of mine. When I saw your daughter, I knew at first blush that I had to have her. It was just something about the way she smiled, showing her perfect set of whites with that sexy gap in the middle."

"Watch it now. You're talking about my baby girl."

"I know, I know. But, Pops, my point is she captured my heart the first time I saw her. After I went and introduced myself to her, she and I started talking a lot over the phone and before we knew it we were going out. I gotta tell you, though, she hated the fact that I sold drugs."

"Did you blame her for hating you for that?"

"No, sir. I didn't. The only thing I blamed her for was compromising what she was taught," Capone replied.

"You hate that my daughter started compromising what she was taught, huh? Whatcha mean by that? Hell, I'm old, you damn near have to explain everything to me," Night-Night's father said.

"There were a lot of things that I was doing that Night-Night initially contested. Some things I do she still contests. But the truth of the matter, Pops, is as the elders of your generation used to say, if you lay down with dogs, you will come up with fleas. I'm not saying that I am a dog, but a lot of things that were, and still are, on me, jumped to her."

"Like what, son?"

"Just street shit in general. Excuse me for cursing."

"Oh, okay. I understand where you're coming from now."

"Honestly though, Pops, I didn't want it to be like that. But after you be around a person for so long, that person's ways start becoming your ways. It's a part of the two people becoming one, I guess."

"Look, like I said, I understand. And trust me, I love my daughter, but I am not the one to be trying to run her life as if she's some type of puppet on a string. She's grown. I did everything I knew to do when she was younger to ensure that she had the things she needed to be equipped for this world we live in. I made sure she had her li'l material things. I made sure her college tuition was paid. All of that. But you know what else I gave her?"

"What's that, Pops?"

"I gave her space. See, I'm not a real religious man, but I do read the Bible. In Genesis, God gave Adam and Eve everything they could ever want. He only commanded them to not do one thing. And that was eating from this particular tree that was in the garden. Did they listen and obey? Hell no! And you wanna know why, son? The reason they didn't listen and obey is because they really wanted to experience something new. Whether good or bad, as long as it's something new, human beings will take their chances on something different from what they had been accustomed to. Up until Adam and Eve had decided to go another way, they had been accustomed to just God and His goodness. When they chose to bite that apple, or whatever fruit they damn ate, that's when they realized beyond a doubt that something other than the goodness of God existed. But you know what? At least God had enough wisdom to give Adam and Eve their space so that they could make whatever decision they wanted to make."

"That makes a lot of sense, Pops," Capone replied thoughtfully.

"I said that to say this: my daughter has chosen you. A guy from the streets. Well, I can identify with that because her mother did the same thing with me. Yes, you heard me right. Her mother did the same thing with me."

"Wait a minute, Pops. Are you telling me that you were a street dude in your day?"

"I wasn't just a street cat. I was knee deep in the heroin game. Made a helluva lot of money. And met the sweetest woman I had ever met when I met my daughter's mother. At the time, she was in the church. She always wore dresses and carried herself different from other girls I had been involved with from the streets. She didn't want to talk to me at all, being that I was a hustler. But, son, I wasn't gonna let her slip away. So, I kept at her and kept at her until she gave in. Then one thing led to another, and before I knew it, I was deeply in love with this woman. And she was in love with me. The only thing that kept her from marrying me at that time was me being in the game. She told me that there was no way she was gonna spend the rest of her life with a drug dealer. She said, 'Either you give that up, or you give me up.' I loved her, but I swear I wasn't ready to give the game up. I was just making too much money.

"But then, son, something happened. I went to make a transaction and was robbed and shot five times in my legs. Two in my left leg and three in the other. It left me wheelchair bound for two and a half months. The whole two and a half months, you know who was there for me, rolling me around, fixing my food, and all that? That woman in that kitchen in there. My wife. She changed my bandages and everything. She proved to me that no dope game deserves the attention that God designed for a man to give his girl. That woman's loyalty to me changed my whole life. After I healed, I had one mission to complete before I said good-bye to the dope game."

"What was that, Pops?" Capone curiously asked.

"I had to see the nigga who robbed and shot me. I just couldn't let that nigga get away. When I got a hold of that nigga, well, let's just say he's history. I've been out the game since. I went legit and started me a construction company. I haven't looked back."

"So, you believe a man can exit the streets, or the game, just like that?" asked Capone.

"It ain't easy. But, son, a man can do anything he puts his mind to. But you have got to have something to fall back on. For me, it was my wife and my construction business, and then came our daughter. Nothing is impossible."

Pops and Capone continued their conversation until they were interrupted by Night-Night who shouted, "Momma, I hate you!" They then saw her coming out of the kitchen where she and her mother were walking fast.

Her mother followed closely behind. "You can hate me all you want, but do it while getting your things so that you and your thug boyfriend there can be on y'all way."

Night-Night stormed into her bedroom to retrieve some of her belongings.

"Now, Lou-Lou, what's the matta now?" Night-Night's father inquired.

His wife looked at him with her hand on her hip. "It's your daughter. She's what's the matter. She's got the devil in her. Ever since this here boyee got out of prison she's been looking strange, acting strange, and talking crazy."

Capone stood up with the quickness. "Ma'am, if you want me to leave, I'll leave."

She pointed to the door. "How fast?" she snapped, giving him the evil eye.

When Capone stood up to leave, she saw that his shirt was poking out at his side. She wasn't stupid. She knew that he had to be carrying a gun.

"Just get out of my house. And I would appreciate it if you never come back."

"No, nooo, now. Wait a minute, son." Night-Night's father stood up. He grabbed a hold of Capone's arm as he was about to walk out the door. "You don't have to go anywhere, son," he said. He then looked over at his wife, who was standing there with her hand on her hip, looking mad.

"Lou-Lou, what has this boy done to you to make you talk to him that way? Now, that's not called for at all."

"In my sight it is. And you shouldn't be asking what has he done to me. You should be asking what has he done to ya daughter," she said.

"Lou-Lou, our daughter is grown."

She looked over at Capone. "Then she ought to act like it. Now, sir, are you gonna get out of my house, or am I gonna have to call the police?"

Capone thought, *Bitch, call the fuck who you want to call. I don't give a damn! Matter of fact, if I weren't so in love with your daughter,*

I would hire two ghetto, ruthless-ass girls to come over here and beat your muthafuckin' ass!

Instead of Capone relaying that thought out loud, he just turned to Night-Night's father. "Nice meeting you again, Pops."

"Nice meeting you again, too, son. Anytime you want to come over and talk with me, feel free to do so."

When his wife heard that, she sighed. "Over my dead body!"

Capone had heard enough. He headed toward the door. "Pops, if you don't mind, please tell your daughter that I'll be waiting for her out here in the driveway."

"He ain't gotta tell me. I'm right behind you," said Night-Night. She walked over to her father first and kissed him. "I'll call you later, Daddy." She then looked over in the direction of her mother. "Momma, I'll see you later."

"Whatever, honey. Whatever."

25

Agent Amy Williams

It was 8:00 a.m. on the dot when Derrick's cell phone started going off. He had two cell phones. But the one that was going off was the one that was given to him by federal agents. "Hello?" he answered.

"Derrick, this is Agent Amy Williams."

"Okay, what's up? 'Cause it's early as fuck."

"I need for you to come to my office soon as possible for some debriefing."

"Debriefing?"

"Yeah. I need to debrief you on some other people."

Derrick sat up in his bed. "Some other people you say? What other people? I told you everything I knew about Fat Jerome. What else is there to tell, Agent Williams?"

"Just get down here to my office as soon as possible. Now, I'll see you when you get here."

Derrick then heard the dial tone. "Dammit! I hate I fuckin' agreed to work with these muthafuckas!" he said, getting up out of his bed. "Now these fuckin' feds think they own a nigga." Derrick was highly upset for having to get up on a fuckin' Friday morning to go debrief. But he had to do what he had to do. However, he would soon find out that everything ain't always what it seems.

When Derrick got to Agent Williams's office, it was a quarter to ten. He watched her as she was the only one in the office. The last time he was there debriefing on his dealings with Fat Jerome, both Agent Williams and her partner, Jonathan Haymaker, were in attendance. Agent Williams escorted Derrick to his seat. Derrick heard a jazz band playing through the ceiling speaker in her office. He didn't recognize the jazz band, but the music they played put a relaxing feeling in the air. *This bitch must be trying to make my ass as comfortable as possible. She must think I got a helluva lot of niggas to tell on. But I ain't telling on nobody but fuckin' Fat Jerome, just as I agreed.*

Next to the wonderful jazz band playing through the ceiling speaker, Derrick noticed something else that caused his ass to do a double take. He noticed how juicy Agent Williams's ass looked. During their previous meetings she wore a long jacket, which made it hard for him to check out her bottom figure. Not that he was trying to do so previously, for she was a federal agent, a woman not really his type of hype. This morning was different though. Not only did Agent Williams's nice, firm, juicy booty catch Derrick's eye, but so did her hairstyle. She had it pinned up with two bangs coming down the side of her face on each side. Her eyebrows were arched perfectly thin, and her blue eyes sparkled as they were highlighted by her eyeliner. Her thin, pointy nose and lips were as those of movie star actress Julia Roberts.

Damn, this redhead FBI agent look sexy as fuck to me this morning. Even the off-brand white khaki shirt that she was wearing exposed her titties. They were nice and small. No more than a good handful, the nipples on them were like little nipples on a baby's bottle. They seemed to be pointing at Derrick as she sat before him to debrief him. The problem was, Derrick didn't know whether to answer her or her titties' nipples.

"Derrick, are you with me this morning? I asked if you knew of a female by the name of Ericka Simpson?"

"Ericka Simpson? Ummm, I don't think I ever heard of her, Agent Williams."

"Here's her picture. Look at it, because you may know her by some other name. You know how you all are in the streets. Y'all have aliases," she said with somewhat of a smile on her face.

Derrick stared at the picture a moment. "Oh, yeah! I know her," he said. "We call her Black Berry. She used to strip in the clubs with my ex-girl Veronda. The two of them were kinda tight."

"So you do know her?"

"Just that she used to strip and shit, that's it," replied Derrick, handing her the picture back.

Agent Williams handed him another picture. "What about this guy?" she asked.

Derrick viewed the picture. "I don't know him at all. Never seen him a day in my life."

"Are you sure, Derrick?" she asked

"I'm as sure as the deodorant," he replied, handing her back the picture. "Who is he?" asked Derrick.

"Samonte Jones, aka Osama."

"I've never seen or met him, but my ex-girl knows of him. She told me once that he was a very vicious man. A killer."

Agent Williams nodded her head up and down. "We believe that he is a killer. In fact, we believe

that he is one of Fat Jerome's number one killers. We have all three of them in the county jail
with no bond: Fat Jerome, Ericka, and Osama.
They all have elected to go to trial. We offered
each of them a plea, but they refused. We were
shocked that Fat Jerome refused, being that we
raided his home and took drugs and major cash
from his property. Instead of cooperating with
us, they all have hired good attorneys to fight for
them. We arrested some others who were a part
of Fat Jerome's crew as well. Some we believe
will eventually cooperate with us. But, Derrick,
we need you to continue to lay low until the trial
is over with."

"I know, and that's exactly what I've been
doing to the best of my ability."

"Well, just keep it up, because we really need
you up on that stand, testifying."

"I gave you my word that I would do it. So,
that's what it's gonna be."

"I believe you. Besides, we got you out of
prison for that purpose."

"You don't even have to remind me. Anyway,
Agent Williams, I wanna ask you something."

"Only if you allow me to ask you something
next," she joked, with a flirtatious smile.

"No problem," Derrick replied. "But check
this out. Eric Brunson, he is a real good friend of

mine. He called my mother's house on the day that I was released. We kicked it about this and that, and he told me among other things that he was facing a lot of time in prison. He also told me that he was cooperating. He didn't talk with me long, but was supposed to call me back. I haven't heard from him since. What's the deal with him? I mean, are you guys gonna see to it that he don't have to do too much time?"

Agent Williams looked at Derrick strangely, as if she had knowledge of something Derrick didn't. She did. "Derrick, the reason you haven't heard from Eric Brunson is because a few months ago he hanged himself in his jail cell."

"Fuck no! That's bullshit," Derrick said in utter disbelief.

"It's the truth. In fact it was all over the local news. Eric Brunson even left a note that read, 'I would rather be dead than spend time in prison.' But the problem with that is Mr. Brunson was supposed to have gotten out much like on a deal you signed. He was gonna be cooperating. The morning he was supposed to have been released, he was found in his cell with a sheet around his neck, hanging from the window pole in his cell. His death is currently under investigation."

"It has to be. Because there is no way on God's green earth that he hanged himself. I could never believe that."

"Well, he was allegedly hustling coke for some Colombians. We don't know much about those people he was working for; it may be possible that they found out that he was gonna cooperate and hired someone to take him out. Someone like a guard or somebody to get to him before he could set the Colombians up for us."

"Who the fuck are the Colombians? Hell, if they are in Charlotte and you guys know where, I'll try to infiltrate their organization. I'll do this shit just on the strength of Eric Brunson being a friend of mine. The guy fuckin' saved my life."

"We don't have a clue as to who these Colombians are, nor their whereabouts. Truth is, we don't even know if they were behind Mr. Brunson committing suicide. The matter is being investigated, like I said."

Derrick sighed. "That's fuckin' crazy. I know he didn't commit suicide. I just know that he didn't do that."

"Well, don't get all worked up about it. I've seen stranger things. Now, if you would allow me, can I please ask you something?"

"You can ask me whatever you want to," Derrick replied.

Agent Williams got up from her seat. She did so to walk across her office to place the pictures that she had previously allowed Derrick to view back into a file drawer that had a combination lock on it. As she walked across that office of hers, she purposely stepped in front of Derrick to do so. The sweet scent from her perfume graced his nostrils. Not to the point of him trying to figure out what the fragrance was, for his eyes were too focused on her booty. Either she was wearing a thong or her ass wasn't wearing any panties at all, Derrick figured. That's how sexy her booty was shaking in her jeans.

As Agent Williams walked across her office, she looked back to see if Derrick had even noticed her switching her ass. When she discovered that he was watching, she blushed.

"So what's the question you want to ask me, Agent Williams?"

Agent Williams waited until she had secured the pictures in the file drawer before responding. She then walked over to Derrick, who was sitting semi slouched in the chair with his legs open wide and both his hands on top of his head. Agent Williams stood before him. She then bent over slightly, facing him. "Tell me, Derrick, is it true that guys who spend time in prison know how to, you know, fuck a woman better than a guy who hasn't been to prison?"

The question caught Derrick totally off guard. This chick was a federal agent. Not some hoochie momma from the hood. However, Derrick respected her boldness. He saw that she was serious. And that most of all, she was curious.

"Here's all your money," said Abdullah. "A whole grand. You can count it." He handed it to a drug dealer.

"Don't worry, I will," replied the dealer he owed. The dealer counted ten one hundred-dollar bills. "It's all here," he said. "Now, what can I do for you?"

"Nothing. I'm straight. But check this out. I just didn't come over here to pay you what I owed, but I'm about to make some changes."

"What type of changes?"

Abdullah put what he had in mind on the line. He had been dealing with this drug dealer for a couple of years. Now it was time to say good-bye. He told him what was about to transpire, then he jumped into his van, tooted him a line of coke, and said to his dealer, "*As-salamu alaykum.*"

"Man, be for real. You ought to stop playing with Allah and Islam, muthafucka."

When the dealer said that, Abdullah took some tissue and wiped his nose. "I'm outta here."

"Burn the road up then, nigga. Fuckin' hypocrite!"

***

Derrick looked Agent Williams directly in her pretty-ass blue eyes. The bitch had freckles on her face and was in her forties. But this morning it was as if her ass was in her twenties. Derrick felt this strongly. He said while watching her, "Yeah, it's fuckin' true. Guys coming home from prison do know how to fuck a woman better than a guy who hasn't been to prison. Especially if that guy did a helluva lot of time."

Agent Williams rubbed her hand over Derrick's crotch. "Really?" she said, with lust all in her fuckin' eyes. "What about the time you did? It wasn't much."

"No, it wasn't much, but it sure as hell felt like a lifetime," Derrick said, licking his lips, cutting her off.

"So, have you had some since you've been home?" she asked, caressing his arousal.

"Nah, not at all. Guess I've just been too busy."

"Really?" she responded, inhaling air through her teeth as she started unbuttoning her shirt. As Derrick suspected, she was braless.

She took hold of one of Derrick's hands and placed it over her left titty. Derrick squeezed and caressed it gently. Then he placed his mouth on her titty. "Yes, that's it. Just . . . just forget that I'm a FBI agent," she said, gripping both sides of his head in pleasure from his warm mouth on her flesh. She didn't have to tell Derrick to forget she was a FBI agent. He had already done that in his mind the moment she placed her hand over his crotch to rub up and down his dick.

Ever since Agent Williams attended college as a teen, majoring in criminal justice, on up to when she graduated from the FBI academy, she had always wanted to feel the dick of a criminal up in her. She often tried shaking this wanting, but to very little avail. Because every time she would have to bust a drug dealer, bank robber, or some type of criminal period, the urges to fuck that individual would spring up in her. If a criminal who had done time inside the joint was getting out, that was even more damn tempting to her. It was more tempting to her because she figured that since the criminal had done time without fuckin' a woman, he had to not only have the energy to last long, but the dick to satisfy her throbbing pussy.

Finally, she had gotten her opportunity. She knew that she would get it the very first day her ass laid eyes on Derrick when she and her partner went to visit him in prison. As she questioned Derrick about his criminal demeanor with Fat Jerome along with her partner, she noticed that when they left, she left with her panties soaked and fuckin' wet. She wanted to fuck Derrick so bad that later that night in her home she finger fucked herself. She had imagined that her finger was Derrick's dick. Imagining such caused her to have one of the biggest damn orgasms she had ever experienced.

Derrick sucked on her titties like he was in a hurry. "Take your time, Derrick. No one is here but you and me. My partner is on vacation," Agent Williams said.

Derrick wet her stomach with his kisses. He then unbuttoned her jeans and pulled them down along with her thong. Agent Williams stepped backward only to ease her ankles and feet from her jeans and thong. Derrick turned her around almost aggressively and bent her over her desk. He removed her hairpin, pulled her hair, and smacked her on her red ass cheek hard. "Ahhh," she moaned. She was already wet. But his thug aggression caused her juices to really flow. "Wait, Derrick. Wait," she said. She turned around to face him and to undress him from the waist down. Derrick noticed that she was slightly trembling. As his Rocawear jean shorts and boxer briefs fell to the floor with her assistance, Agent William's eyes got big. She couldn't believe that his dick was the size that it was. *Damn, he must've been jacking his dick a lot while in prison for it to be this long and thick.* She just had to put her mouth on it. "Can I suck your cock, Derrick?"

Unless there's a law against you suckin' my dick in this here office of yours, Agent Williams, you can. If there was a law prohibiting such, Agent Williams would have turned criminal herself and broken the muthafucka, because nothing was gonna stop her from coming face to face with Derrick's dick and taking advantage of suckin' it like it was her favorite piece of candy.

"You can do whatever you want to do with it, Agent Williams," Derrick lustfully muttered, running his fingers through her hair.

"Please, you don't have to call me Agent Williams. Call me Amy."

"Okay, Amy. And you don't have to call me Derrick. Call me Cobra."

She placed her whole mouth over his dick. She damn near choked, trying to deep throat the muthafucka. She moved her mouth back and forth on it. The warmth and wetness of her mouth, and the way she tightened her jaws while his dick was in her mouth, gave him a sensation that not even good dick suckin' from his ex-girlfriend Veronda could match. *What the fuck this bitch doing working for the damn FBI as good and wonderful as she sucks a dick?*

Her ass should be a fuckin' call girl somewhere in Vegas. Derrick threw his head back, closed his eyes, and took in air through his teeth. "Lord have mercy, Amy, it feels as if I've died and gone to damn heaven with this good-ass dick suckin' you delivering," he moaned, completely satisfied with what she was doing to him.

"I'm glad you're enjoying yourself," she responded. She then eased up. "Bend me over and fuck the hell out of me. Fuck me like you've been in prison for twenty years without any contact at all between a woman's legs." Derrick bent her ass over aggressively. "Yes, that's it, Cobra."

Derrick then spanked her, while pulling her hair. "Oh, gossh yess. Now put that big cock of yours in me," she shamelessly moaned. Derrick parted her legs with his right leg and foot while she was bent over her desk. The pretty li'l red hairs around her pussy from the back made his dick harder than the great dick suckin' she had just delivered to him. He thrust his rod deep inside her with one forceful thrust. "Ahhhh," she screamed, while at the same time, squirming upward on her desk. A folder with all types of documents fell to the floor along with ink pens as she squirmed upward. With nowhere to go, she buried her nails from both hands into the side of his thighs. Derrick was pounding her pussy hard and pulling her hair.

"This is what you been needing in your life, isn't it?" Derrick said, as he went in and out of her, the thug way.

"Yesses," she screamed. "Harder, puhleeze." All Agent Williams could think about while Derrick's long, thick dick was deep up in her was how much she had longed for this pleasurable moment. The feeling she was experiencing sent all types of sexual sensitive shockwaves all through her damn body, enough for Derrick to see from the white creamish foam all over his dick that she had nutted extremely hard. He had done the same.

When it was over, Agent Williams looked at Derrick. "Whatever you do, don't ever tell anyone about what happened in my office. If you keep your mouth shut about this, you can get it anytime I'm available. Is that a deal?"

"That's a deal," replied Derrick reassuringly.

He was about to walk out of her office until she said, "Oh, yeah. I got something else for you."

"What's that?"

She tossed him a pair of handcuffs. "Next time, I want you to use those."

This woman is a freak for real.

"That's not what I got for you, though. What I really have for you is this." She handed Derrick a piece of paper with a phone number written on it.

"What is this? Your phone number?" Derrick asked.

"That's the number to someone dying to talk to you. Call it as soon as possible."

"Well, who is it?"

"Can't tell you. But I am sure you will want to have a word or two with the person."

26

How The Hell Is It You Don't Know My Voice?

Derrick left Agent Amy Williams's office and headed back home. "Put On" by rapper Young Jeezy was pumpin' hard as hell through his car speakers, causing him to bob his head to its hardcore street beat and lyrics. He cruised through the city on his way home, feeling good as a muthafucka. He had just laid pipe to an older white sexy chick, who was not only a fuckin' freak, but a damn sworn-in FBI agent. The scent from sexing her was still heavily on him. Freshening up was his only concern at the moment. Next to this concern, another one lingered on his mind heavily. It was the number that Agent Williams had given him. He grabbed his cell phone, flicked it open, and dialed the number.

After four rings he heard a female voice say, "Pamela speaking."

Pamela? Who the fuck is Pamela? Derrick thought before saying, "Ah, yes. I really don't know how to say this, but I was told that someone at this number wanted to speak with me?"

"Well, who are you?" she asked, pretending not to know.

"Derrick. My name is Derrick."

"Derrick?" she repeated. "That's it? No middle names, no last name? Just Derrick, huh?"

"Oh, I'm sorry, ma'am. It's Derrick Bellamy."

"No need for apologies. Just need for clarity that's all. Clarity. Besides, the Derrick Bellamy I know would never apologize for not doing something majorly wrong."

"So you know me?" Derrick curiously asked.

"Maybe."

"Who are you?"

"I'm Pamela. But I already told you that."

"Pamela who? 'Cause I don't know any Pamelas. The only Pamela I ever heard of is the TV star."

"Well, I ain't white with blond hair and blue eyes. This here pretty and light skin, baby."

"Okay, I feel you, but I don't know you."

"Just say you don't know my name. Even so, though, you should know my voice, Derrick."

Derrick thought a moment. The voice sounded familiar, but he just couldn't make out who it was. Rather than make a mistake, he just said, "Are you gonna tell me who you are? Or are you gonna kick my ass with this guessing game?"

Pamela felt a little hurt. *How could he not recognize my voice after all the damn time he and I spent together?* She then eased his curious mind.

"Nigga, this Veronda! How the hell is it you don't know my voice, Derrick?"

"Ohhhh, shit! My muthafuckin' baby girl. What the fuck?"

"Your baby girl, my ass. How can I be your baby girl and you forgot what my voice sounds like and shit?"

"I swear, I knew this Pamela chick you were claiming to be sounded like you. I just didn't want to fuckin' call your name out and be wrong. Damn, though, girl. Where the fuck you been?"

"Man, I was in the ATL trying to get my damn self established and shit, then what do you know, here comes the fuckin' feds knockin' at my door late one night."

"Say what?"

"Hell yeah. When they fuckin' introduced themselves I thought I had a warrant or something for my arrest. Come to find out these muthafuckas came to save my ass."

"They came to save you?" Derrick repeated, confused. "Save you from what?"

"Not save me from what. Save me from whom. How about Fat Jerome had sent Osama and that damn fake-ass friend of mine, Ericka, up here to kill me."

"Damn!" Derrick said.

"The feds intercepted their attempt though."

"How in the hell did the feds know about it?"

"They fuckin' know everything. And I really shouldn't be telling you this on the phone and shit, but fuck it, it is what it is. They had Fat Jerome's house and phone bugged. They played the damn tape for me and everything. Osama was coming to blow my damn brains out and Ericka with her fake ass was gonna set the shit up."

"Damn, that's who always end up crossing you, your own muthafuckin' friends. The niggas you think would actually have your back and shit."

"I can't wait to take the stand on them niggas. And I ain't no rat. But thanks to the feds, them bitches hit and missed. Now it's my turn. If I have anything to do with it, all of them getting life sentences."

"So you cooperating?"

"You goddamn right! And from what I heard, so are you. What brought you to this point?"

When Veronda asked Derrick that, his phone started beeping. "Hold on, Veronda, let me check my line." Derrick clicked over. "Hello?"

"Derrick, where are you? You just up and left this morning without saying a word."

"I'm pulling up right now, Momma, in the driveway. Everything's all right."

"Well, I'm just checkin' to see."

"Everything's fine, Momma. Now, I'll be inside in one moment."

"Okay then. Bye."

Derrick clicked back over to Veronda. "I'm back," he said.

"So, back to my question. What brought you to the point of wanting to cooperate with the feds? They told me that you didn't have but a gun charge."

"The gun charge didn't have anything to do with it. It was my little brother."

"The little birthday boy?" asked Veronda.

"Yeah, with your crazy self." Derrick knew what was on Veronda's mind. She was reflecting on the day she gave Mike-Mike some head at Derrick's request.

"Nah, Derrick, you're the one crazy," she said, laughing.

"Well, the feds showed me a picture of him on the goddamn block, selling coke."

"Bullshit. Not your little brother. Hell nah."

"Real talk, Veronda. The worst part about it was his ass sold a couple bags to a damn undercover cop. They didn't lock his ass up though, thank God. But after the feds showed me that shit, I was like, 'I got to get the fuck out of prison and save my li'l fuckin' brother. I can't have his ass on no damn corner on his way to prison.'"

"Shit, I know that's right," Veronda agreed.

"So I just went on ahead and told the feds what they wanted to know and they got my ass out of prison. I still got to take the stand though on Fat Jerome. But fuck it, I don't give a damn about that fat muthafucka."

"Why should you give a damn about him?"

"Not just that, Veronda. But my moms. She started battling with breast cancer while I was in the joint. She's getting better now. But I swear when I came home, she looked like a totally different person. That cancer shit ain't no joke. Her hair is just starting to grow back."

"Is she a'ight now though?"

"She's getting better."

"I know that y'all had moved because when I was in Atlanta, I had written you several times, but all my letters came back."

"I was in the joint then. I swear, I was stressing like a muthafucka over you. Every day I thought about you. But I figured after not hearing from you at all, maybe you had just gone on with your life."

"Never, Derrick. Never. Just like you thought about me I thought about you. I didn't even date niggas while in Atlanta."

"C'mon now, Veronda. You telling me that you didn't allow them niggas down there to get some of that good pussy?"

"Hell fuckin' no! I was determined to not fuck any nigga I wasn't in love with. Fuck that shit."

"You didn't date or nothing?"

"I didn't even date, Derrick, and that's the honest to God truth. I guess I was hoping that my Prince Charming would come to Atlanta and rescue me from my loneliness. Because I was definitely lonely without you. No bullshit! What about you? Did you find you someone else?"

"Shit, I went to the joint."

"Yeah, but you've been out of the joint for a little while now. Is there someone special?"

Derrick thought about the encounter that he had just had with Agent Amy Williams. She had provided him with one of the best damn dick sucks he had ever experienced. It was his first since he had been out of prison. Having access to Agent Williams's goods from here on out for his pleasure as well as hers was a treat worthy of not turning down. Because next to having some good-ass head she had a pussy between her legs that was wet and felt good and tight enough for him to know that there weren't a lot of miles on it. His encounter with her blew his mind, but didn't capture his heart. Veronda, and Veronda alone, had that. And speaking with her again reinforced it.

"I haven't found anyone as special as you, Veronda. You are the only girl I have ever wanted to really spend the rest of my life with. Straight up, boo."

Veronda blushed while holding her phone. She then said, "So you still love me, huh?"

"I never stopped loving you. Now, look, I gotta get ready to go so that I can take me a fuckin' shower and run across town. Is there any way we can see each other?"

"The feds want me keepin' a low profile, Derrick. They don't want me being seen and shit all in the city."

"I can dig that. They want me keeping my head low and shit too."

"Nevertheless, Derrick, check this out. Give me a number where I can reach you, and I'll hit you back in a few hours with where we might be able to meet up. Shit, it's Friday."

"Bet," replied Derrick. He gave Veronda his number and told her to make sure that she called him later. Derrick then disconnected their conversation and headed inside.

27

You Upset 'Cause You Wanna Be

Capone hit the gas hard on his way out of Night-Night's mother and father's driveway. He was mad as hell at how Night-Night's mother treated his ass. He was so upset at the moment that he saw himself in his mind's eye pistol whipping the hell out of Night-Night's mom.

Night-Night knew that he was highly upset. Hell, it was written all over his damn face. So she remained quiet. Instead of saying something that might provoke him further to anger, she placed her favorite old-school song, "If It Isn't Love" by New Edition, inside the CD player and pushed play. As the music was playing she turned up the volume, and then laid her head back on the seat's headrest, in hopes of enjoying her song. But Capone wasn't having it. He reached down and turned the volume down. He turned the volume down so low, Night-Night could hardly hear it.

"Whatcha doin', baby? That's my favorite song. I want to hear it," she said, turning it back up.

"I don't wanna hear any music right now, Night-Night," Capone said, turning it down again.

"What that got to do with me?" she growled. She then moved his hand, and turned the volume up. This time she turned the volume up louder than it was when she first put the song on. This made Capone furious. He reached over and smacked the shit out of her. The smack was so hard and loud that it could be heard over the music, and the music was damn near at the max.

Night-Night grunted in pain and cupped her jaw. "That shit hurts. Why you slap me, Capone?"

"'Cause yo' ass act like you can't fuckin' hear."

"So fuckin' what! That don't give your ass a right to fuckin' slap me," she snapped, starting to cry. "I ain't did shit to you. You just want to take your damn anger out on me."

"Look! I ain't tryin'a hear it, a'ight! I ain't tryin'a hear shit!" Capone barked.

Night-Night didn't back down. She cut the CD player completely off. After he had smacked the shit out of her, he had turned it down a third time. But now she was just as upset as he was.

After turning it off, she looked at him sternly. "No! You gon' listen to me! 'Cause you have never hit me before. Why fuckin' now, Capone, huh?"

"Because your li'l ass hardheaded." When Capone said that, Night-Night reached over and smacked the shit out of his face as he had done to hers. He damn near ran into a nearby car on the highway.

"Watch where the fuck you're going, dammit!" shouted the driver he nearly ran into.

"Night-Night, I'ma beat yo' ass. Just wait 'til we get to the damn hotel."

"We'll just be beating each other's ass 'cause, nigga, you know better than to ever put your hands on me. Whatever happened to what you told me a long time ago, huh? About you wouldn't ever hit me?"

"I'm fuckin' upset! A'ight? Why you just can't shut your damn pie hole? I just wanted a little quiet time. That's all I wanted, Night-Night."

"You upset 'cause you wanna be."

"No! I'm fuckin' upset because your damn momma thinks she knows every goddamn thing! She don't fuckin' know me. Why the hell you think I didn't want to go over there from the start?"

"We already went through that, Capone. And it makes no difference how much my mother or anyone else for that matter hates you. No one can make you upset if you don't allow them to."

"Shit, that's easy for you to say. She doesn't hate you. She hates me."

"She hates my decision to be with you, all the same. So don't fuckin' use that as an excuse. I wanted you to come with me over to my mother and father's house because, hell, we go everywhere else to-damn-gether."

"Going to the mall or going out to eat is different from going to your mother's house. That woman sees me as Satan himself. She's crazy."

"Damn how she sees you! Who yo' woman? Huh? Me or her?"

"You don't expect me to damn answer that do you?"

"I'm just fuckin' saying."

"Saying fuckin' what?" asked Capone.

Night-Night sighed. "Baby, I'm just fuckin' saying that if you're angry and bent all out of shape, don't take it out on me. I love you. And you and I are in this together, remember?"

"I just don't like being rejected without a real strong, justifiable reason."

"Baby, not all people are gonna see you in the light and view that you would wish they would. That's fuckin' life. That's the way it is."

"So, what, I'm supposed to act like I'm not affected by rejection? I ain't no damn phony."

"And I ain't calling you one. You gotta be you, baby, and only you."

"A'ight then."

"Just don't be taking your damn anger out on someone who doesn't deserve it."

"Well, from now on don't be damn coercing me to go places I don't wanna go," said Capone.

After Capone said that, Night-Night looked up and noticed that they were in North Charlotte. Capone immediately spotted a nigga who he knew for a fact was down with Fat Jerome's crew. The nigga was on the corner alone, selling coke.

"What are we doing over here, Capone?" asked Night-Night. She saw Capone lift his gun from his waist and set it on his lap.

"Just when I get out to handle my business, take over the wheel."

Before Night-Night could contest, Capone drove straight up to the corner where this guy was hustling. He stopped right in front of him and got out with his gun in hand.

"Muthafucka, empty your goddamn pockets!" Capone said with his gun at the nigga's temple. The nigga lifted both his hands in panic.

"Ca . . . Capone, what's goin' on, mannn?"

"Muthafucka, what? You didn't hear me? I said, empty yo' goddamn pockets!"

Capone smacked the nigga in the forehead with his gun, ensuring that he got the message this time. It worked. "A'ight, dawg. Take everything," the nigga said.

He was bleeding profusely from the head. He was handing Capone coke and knots of money from every pocket. "Hurry the fuck up, muthafucka!" Capone spat, hitting him again over the head. This time, the nigga fell flat out unconscious. Capone picked through the nigga's pockets and took everything he had. He then stood over him and thought about his brother, Rasco. "Y'all niggas killed my little brother."

"Baby, c'mon before we end up in a fuckin' shootout, now," shouted Night-Night with the passenger's side door open for him to jump in. He pretended not to hear her. Instead, he continued standing over the nigga he'd just robbed and knocked unconscious. He started beating the nigga in his head with his gun. He beat the nigga until blood was all over his gun and his face.

Capone had zoned out, and was determined to take this guy's life, until he heard an old lady yell, "Somebody call the police! That boy over there gon' kill that boy! Somebody puhleeze call the police."

That's when Capone came to and jumped into his Escalade, and Night-Night skidded off. The nigga Capone had just finished beating down was left on the corner like a rag doll, with blood all over him.

"Damn, baby, what you go and do that shit for?" asked Night-Night as she hit the nearest highway.

"It was the only way I was gonna get over my anger. I had to get it out. Besides, fuck Fat Jerome and them niggas!"

Night-Night couldn't contest. Neither did she want to at this point. She was in love with a bad boy. And if she didn't know anything else, she knew that sometimes bad boys do bad-ass things.

28

I Waited Long Enough!

In a rented money green Range Rover, Derrick and Veronda met in Monroe, North Carolina. Derrick drove his car there to the only Hardee's in that small town. It only took him forty-five minutes to get where Veronda had told him to meet her. Once there, Derrick parked his car, and got into the money green Range Rover with Veronda.

The moment he got inside, she was all over him like white on rice. "Damn, baby, I missed the hell out of you," she uttered in between kisses. Her pussy got wet as H_2O just at the sight of Derrick. She saw that he had picked up a little weight. Not fat, though. All muscle. His hair was cut short in a Caesar, with waves all around it in beehive fashion. He was wearing a white wife beater, exposing his muscular shoulders, arms, and biceps, and doo-doo brown Sean John sweat pants, with the all-white high-top Air Force Ones. Veronda just wanted to eat him up; he looked so sexy. So was she to him. She had her hair down. It had gotten longer since he last saw her.

In fact, it was now down to her lower back. She was wearing a hot-pink Baby Phat skintight full-body skirt. He loved it when she wore skirts like that because they exposed her thick thighs and sexy muscular calves. She also had on some cute pink and white Air Max Nikes. As they tongued kissed the hell out of each other, Veronda placed Derrick's hand between her thighs. Her thighs were warm to Derrick's touch. He eased his hand up her skirt and was surprised that he had easy access to her pussy because she wasn't wearing any panties. He looked her in the eyes. "Damn, girl, you want me just as bad as I want you, huh?"

"I waited long enough. Don't you think?" she replied, with her eyes slightly closed at him massaging her clit. She was dripping wet, and he was massively hard. He flicked her clit faster and faster while they kissed. "Oh, gosh, Derrick that feels goooood," she moaned.

"You like that, baby?" Derrick said. His finger was soaking wet with her juices.

"I love it. Don't stop."

"I got to, baby," said Derrick. He stopped flicking her clit fast.

"Why, baby? Why you gotta stop?"

"'Cause I want to fuck," he declared.

"Right here, Derrick? Right here in this parking lot?"

"Hell yeah! Shit, ain't nobody paying us any attention. It's nighttime anyway. Plus, the windows are tinted. Now, come over here and straddle me."

Derrick hit the button on the side of his seat. The part where his back and head rested went backward in slow motion, causing him to be laid flat on his back like he was in a bed. He then eased down his sweats and underwear. When he did Veronda got a good look at his dick and took in a deep breath with enlarged eyes. It looked as if his dick had grown a few inches since their last encounter. She got on top of him with her skirt up at her waist. He firmly gripped her ass cheeks. They were just as soft as they were prior to her going off to Atlanta. "Gosh, I missed the hell out of you, Derrick. You still crazy as hell, too. You know that?" she said as she kissed his ears, face, and neck.

"Crazy about you. That's the only thing crazy about me," he said. He then slid his dick, hard as a rock, up in her. She was tight, so he let her come down on it at her on pace. As she was taking all of it up in her, Derrick was looking her in her eyes.

She could hardly open them. The only thing open on her face was her mouth as if she was about to scream out loud from his dick being buried deep within her. She slowly ground on Derrick's dick. All he could do was squeeze her ass cheeks tight and assist her in grinding her hips in a circular motion and up and down his dick, while he closed his eyes. If Veronda didn't have anything else in this world, she had some good-ass pussy. She had the type of pussy that would make a man wanna go home and slap his mother! It was wet, juicy, and tight. He smacked Veronda's ass cheeks as she moved up and down on his dick. Her soft flesh jiggled in his hand like it was Jell-O pudding.

Veronda was moaning and groaning loud and long with every grind. "Mmmmm, baby," she moaned. "This your pussy."

"It is, baby girl?"

"Mmmm, hmmmm. Please don't ever let it get away from you again."

Veronda moaned. She was cummin' and so was he. She came so hard, she damn near collapsed on him. Her whole damn body was trembling uncontrollably. At that moment, Derrick held her tight. "Baby, when this damn trial shit is over, we gotta get us a place together. We don't need to leave each other again. I love you," he said. "I really do fuckin' love you, Veronda."

Spanky was the name of the young cat Capone had utterly beat down with his gun and robbed. He was now over in Carolina Medical Center in a coma and not expected to live. The blows from the .357 Magnum that Capone kept hitting Spanky with over his head were more than any man could stand. Two of Spanky's cousins were down from Philly. They were twins named Mooky and Pooky. Both were street cats with vicious reputations as killers in South Philly. They were only in Charlotte on business. Things were getting hot up in South Philly, so Spanky told them to come to Charlotte and think about setting up shop down there. The two of them had just left Spanky to go to the mall. Spanky didn't want to go. He told them that he had money to make and that he would be on the block when they returned. When they returned, family members and friends informed them that Spanky had been beaten and robbed. Now, here they were, both Mooky and Pooky, at Carolina Medical Center, furious.

They were determined to get the nigga who had done this to their cousin no matter the cost. It just so happened that a guy who had seen everything from a distance had followed Mooky and Pooky to the hospital. The guy spotted the twins in the lobby.

"Yo, I watched the whole damn thing, dawg, from a distance. Nigga just jumped out of his Escalade and put his gun to Spanky's head. I saw Spanky coming out of his pockets with everything. The nigga then started beating Spanky something bad, dawg. I wanted to intervene and shit."

"Why the fuck didn't you?" Mooky growled, stepping up in the dude's face.

But Pooky looked at his brother. "Chill, nah, man."

"Let me find out one you niggas set my fuckin' cousin up. I ain't gon' be nothing nice, I swear on my mother, yo," said Mooky angrily.

"Man, Spanky a'ight with me. I was just too far away. But I know the nigga who did the shit."

"What's his name?"

"Nigga's name Capone. He ain't nothing to play with. Trust me."

"How the fuck you know him like that?"

"'Cause he used to hang out over here all the time before he went to prison. Prior to that, he was a notorious stick-up kid. His brother Rasco was a killa. He dead though."

"How can we find this nigga, yo?"

"I know where you can find him. See, I followed his Escalade, 'cause for real, I was thinking about confronting him about beating Spanky down like that. But I didn't want to take any chances with that nigga. But check it, he and some chick staying at the Radisson Hotel."

"Do me a favor and show me and my brother. That's all we want you to do."

"Man, I would take pleasure in doing that shit. Because, like I said, that nigga didn't have to beat Spanky down like that. Spanky don't bother nobody."

"Just show us where this nigga living. That's all I want you to do," Mooky concluded. His brother nodded in agreement with a mean-ass grin on his face.

Before they all left, Mooky and Pooky went up to visit their cousin Spanky. The dude who had witnessed Spanky getting beat down couldn't see him. The doctors only allowed family to see him. Spanky was damn near unrecognizable. He had tubes everywhere. It didn't look like he was gonna make it. Mooky grabbed hold of Spanky's hand and squeezed it tight. A tear fell down his cheek. "Hold on, cousin. Hold on."

29

I Was With Veronda

Derrick busted off twice in Veronda in the damn parking lot of Hardee's. Both of them then went and checked into a hotel room and continued what they had started. They fucked, made love, and caught up on a helluva lot of stuff that they needed to talk about. When Derrick got back home, it was almost two o'clock in the morning. He saw his mother knocked out on the living room sofa. The television was still on, and the remote was still being gripped tightly by his mother's hand.

Derrick walked over and kissed his mother on her forehead. When he did so her eyes opened slowly. "Mmmm, Derrick, what time is it?" she asked.

"A little to two."

"You just getting in?"

"Yes, ma'am. I had to see someone I hadn't seen in a while." He gently grabbed the remote from her hand.

"This late, Derrick?" she said, getting up from the sofa slowly.

"I didn't expect to come home this late, Momma. But I was with Veronda and lost track of time."

"You were with Veronda? I thought you didn't know where she was."

"I didn't. Someone else who I have been in touch with did." Derrick never told his mother about how he had agreed to testify on a drug dealer to get out of prison. Matter of fact, his mother never even questioned how he was released before his initial release date. She was just glad he was home. That's why he didn't choose to mention that FBI Agent Amy Williams gave him Veronda's phone number.

"Well, how is she doing?" his mother asked, making her way toward her bedroom.

"She's fine, Momma. We just had a lot to catch up on."

His mother looked at him up and down. "I'll bet the two of you did," she said, smiling.

"Momma, you something else. So, are you feeling okay?"

"I feel fine, just a little tired, that's all."

"Get you some rest then, and I'll talk to you in the morning." He walked over and kissed her cheek. "I love you, Momma, a'ight?"

"Ummm, hmmm," his mother uttered.

Derrick took a nice hot bath. While he sat in the tub, he thought long and hard about Veronda. She still was so beautiful to him. After a year and a half of not being with her at all, he was still in love with her. And it was apparent to him as well that she was still in love with him. He looked down at his lower chest and stomach and saw that Veronda had left hickey marks all over his body. That was her way of claiming ownership of him. She was still the sweet, sexy girl he was dying to meet years ago at the strip club. When he saw her on stage doing her thing, he knew beyond a shadow of a doubt that he had to have her. After her show was over, he met with her in the parking lot, introduced himself, and then asked if he could take her to IHOP. That's where all the players and ballers went after club hours were over.

Veronda liked his manners and thought he was cute as a muthafucka. So, she allowed herself to go on that date with him. That date led to other dates. Then, finally, before Derrick knew it, he and Veronda were doing more hanging out together than she was strippin'. When she discovered that Derrick was selling dope and that his connection had to leave Charlotte, she turned him on to Fat Jerome, who she was doing certain little things for, like delivering heroin packages off to this location and that location. Derrick started making big money fuckin' with Fat Jerome. He was making more money than any of his friends.

Damn, that fat muthafucka had to go and sedate my baby and then fuck her up her ass without her damn permission. We could be still making a helluva lot of money, this fat nigga and me. I guess that's just the way it is sometimes. Shit, some things just aren't meant to be.

One thing that was meant to be as far as his heart was concerned at the moment was him and Veronda being together. They were back in touch with each other. And in Derrick's mind, the reconnection couldn't have been just coincidental.

He finished his bath and prepared to crash. When he checked his cell phone, he discovered that Agent Williams had been trying to contact him.

The next day, which was Saturday, Derrick returned Agent Williams's call. It was 1:15 p.m. according to his watch. He held the phone to his ear while nodding his head to "Can't Tell Me

Nothing" by Kanye West. Agent Williams phone rang six times before he heard her answer, "Good afternoon. Agent Williams speaking."

"Agent Williams, this is Derrick."

"Oh, hi, Derrick. I was trying to contact you yesterday."

"I know. But I was out last night and didn't have my phone on me."

"Derrick, you must keep that phone on you at all times. We told you that from the beginning. It's the only way for us to know if you're okay."

"I know. I just forgot, Agent Williams," Derrick lied. Truth was, he didn't want to be bothered by anyone while he was with Veronda. And Agent Williams . . . Well, it was true that the FBI wanted to know of Derrick's whereabouts at all times being that he was an informant. But Agent Williams's concern was getting her some more dick.

Had Derrick returned her call last night, she would have met him somewhere other than her office and fucked him. She wasn't gonna cry over spilled milk though. Since she was alone at her office again, and had Derrick on the phone, she said to him, "I need for you to come see me."

"You mean now?" replied Derrick.

"Yes. Like within the next thirty or forty minutes."

Derrick rushed over to Agent Williams's office like he was in a race for a prize. He thought that she was calling him over to her office to tell him that the FBI followed him last night to the parking lot of Hardee's and discovered him and Veronda fuckin' like rabbits. Nothing could have been further from the truth, though. When he got into her office and she shut that office door of hers behind him, he was surprised when she grabbed him by the collar and started tongue kissing him aggressively.

He could hardly breathe, she was coming on so strong.

"Mmmm. Mmmm. Mmmmm," she moaned between kisses.

Derrick finally backed his lips away from hers. "Are you all right, Agent Williams?"

She removed her blouse. Derrick saw her nice pretty red titties jump up and down when she did so. "Just fuck me, please. That's all I want." She removed her jeans, and then walked back up to Derrick. She dropped to her knees before him, only to unzip his fly so that she could have access to his dick. She pulled it out. It was semihard.

But when she graced it with her tongue and mouth, it stood upright, throbbin'. Before Derrick knew it, he was coming out of his damn shorts while she was deep throating his dick. He practically had to back his dick out of her mouth just so that he could take his shorts and underwear off. He then bent her over on the floor of her office doggie style. "Grab those handcuffs off of my desk please and cuff me before you fuck me," Agent Williams said. Derrick grabbed the cuffs and put them on her like he was about to arrest a bad girl. Her back was deeply arched and her ass was tooted upward, high. All Derrick could see was pussy, pussy, pussy. She looked backward at him and beheld his big dick. "Fuck the hell out of me with that juicy, long cock of yours, Cobra. I don't care how loud I scream; don't have any mercy on me. Please don't."

I got a fuckin' pain freak on my hands. He then placed two fingers in her pussy. It was drippin' wet, which was all he wanted to know. He then placed his dick at her tunnel and entered. The more his dick grew inside her, the more she tried moving and squirming upward and moaning loudly. Derrick grabbed her by the handcuffs that bound her hands together and started pounding his dick up in her. He fucked her so hard and good, she started crying and calling him daddy.

He knew from studying black history while in prison that fuckin' a white woman in slavery days was prohibited. If a black man was caught with a white woman, his ass would be beaten severely then killed. Times had changed. He was fuckin' the goddamn shit out of Agent Williams. "Whose pussy is this now?" Derrick said, pounding his dick in and out of her.

"Yourrrs," she screamed. "It's all yours."

Every time Derrick thrust his dick up in her, her ass cheeks bounced. He loved it when they did this. It made his dick even harder. He started smacking her ass cheeks with his open palm hard simultaneously as he fucked her. "Are you gonna tell your partner that I'm fuckin' you like this?" asked Derrick.

"Noooo," she shamelessly moaned.

"You gon' tell the prosecutor?"

"Nooo, daddy."

"You gon' tell the judge?"

"Noo."

"Who the fuck you gon' tell, then?" Derrick continued to question, while fuckin' her harder and faster. He was feeling himself about to cum.

"Nobody, daddy. I ain't gon' tell nobody." She then started screaming loud. "Oh, oh, oh, myyyy Goddddd." Her whole body was shaking. Derrick pulled out of her and nutted all over her ass cheeks. "That's it, daddy, write your name on it, then put it back in."

She and Derrick continued to fuck until Derrick fucked her little freaky white ass dry. She couldn't believe how much stamina Derrick had. When they had finished, they dressed and she kissed Derrick. "I saw those marks on your chest," she said, "and I'm jealous. I know you fucked Veronda last night. You know us FBI agents know everything. I just want me some on a regular basis. I love that big cock of yours. I simply love it, and can't help myself," she said, gripping his dick.

"Now, before you leave, I thought I'd inform you that Fat Jerome and the rest of them have filed for a speedy trial, so get ready to take the stand soon."

"No problem," Derrick replied. As Agent Williams walked him to the door, he noticed that she was walking damn near knock-kneed. *I fucked the hell out her ass. Tore that pussy up!*

It must have been fate, because Derrick had no idea of the information that was about to hit him like a damn slug from a shotgun as he pumped gas in his car. He had just left Agent Amy Williams's office. When he noticed that his gas tank was on E, he stopped by the nearest gas station available to him. As he was finishing up pumping his gas, a guy walked directly up to him, and said, "Yo, bro, aren't you that dude I saw talking with Abdullah, the guy who be selling clothes and shit?"

Derrick didn't know whether to answer this guy. *This nigga might be connected to Fat Jerome; if he find out who I am, he might blow my fuckin' brains out. I don't even have a fuckin' gun or nothing.* Not to mention the dude looked thugged out, with cornrows and gold fronts in his mouth. Derrick saw that he was driving a dark blue chromed-out 5.0 Mustang Saleen, with a fine-ass redbone chick on the passenger's side.

"Yeah, you saw me talking to him?" Derrick went ahead and replied.

When Derrick said that, he saw the guy quickly reach at his waistband and lift his shirt to retrieve something. Derrick was about to run for cover, thinking that it was a gun. But when he saw that the guy was retrieving his cell phone, he relaxed. Apparently, the guy had a call coming in. He looked at his cell phone then pushed a button and placed it back at his side. "I just knew you looked familiar," the guy said. "That's a nice-ass, chromed-out, old-school candy apple red Chevy Impala you got there. So, you must've been serving Abdullah too, huh?"

Derrick looked at the guy strange. "Whatcha mean by that, dawg?"

"That coke. Abdullah loved the fuck outta some powder cocaine. And you look like the type of cat who might be hustling."

"Been there, done that. But, ah, you saying that Abdullah, who be selling the clothes and whatnot, get high?" inquired Derrick.

"Man, what? You don't know? That nigga love that cocaine. I kept his ass in my damn pockets. He won't be selling clothes down here in Charlotte anymore though."

"Why you say that, dawg?" Derrick curiously asked.

"Shit, that's what his ass told me a couple days ago before he left to go to New York."

"He told you that he ain't coming back to Charlotte?"

"That's exactly what he told me. I didn't give a fuck though. All I was glad about was the nigga paying me my muthafuckin' grand."

Derrick lifted his head and looked to the sky. *I know damn well that muthafucka didn't take my goddamn money. I gave that son of a bitch ten fuckin' grand! I know he didn't just do me like that.* "Fuck!"

The guy looked at Derrick. "What's wrong, dawg? The nigga Abdullah owed you some clothes, didn't he? I know he promised your ass something."

Derrick kept the matter to himself. "Just tell me, do you know where that nigga at in New York?"

"Fuck no. That fake-ass Muslim could be anywhere. All that nigga does is lie. If his ass wouldn't have paid me when he did, I was coming over to that car wash where I saw you talking to him, and was gonna put some hot lead in his chest. No bullshit! You can't play with these niggas out here in these streets, dawg. Shit, 'cause everything ain't always what it seems. I'ma let you go though, bro, 'cause I got my girl in the car waiting on me. Just thought I'd holler at you, 'cause you looked familiar. Plus, I wanted to compliment you on that nice-ass ride."

Derrick gave the dude some dap, and then they parted company. Derrick was so damn upset that he didn't even take the guy's name; neither did Derrick give the guy his. He jumped into his ride with all types of thoughts racing through his head. Among those thoughts was the harsh reality that he had been fuckin' suckered by a smooth criminal. And there was nothing his ass could do about it.

He got home and thought about the matter more. He elected not to share it with his mother though, because he knew that she would only tell him that everything that glitters ain't gold. Although that would be an absolutely true statement and damn good advice, sometimes the truth hurts so bad that at the moment of its delivery all an individual wants to do is turn a deaf ear to it to his own detriment.

Derrick chalked his ten grand up as a loss. The thought of getting suckered pained him on a daily basis though. Next time, he wouldn't be so anxious. If he didn't learn nothing else from getting beat, he learned he was still young and had much more to learn about life, and people.

30

You A Dead Muthafucka

"Baby, I didn't know you ordered pizza," Night-Night shouted to Capone. He was in the shower with the bathroom door shut and could barely hear her.

"What you say, Night-Night?" he shouted back in reply.

By that time, Night-Night was opening their hotel room door. *Capone always damn doing something without consulting with me. Hell, I'm tired of eating damn pizza. It's pizza in the morning, pizza in the afternoon, and damn pizza in the fuckin' late night like this. Shit I want me a steak and mashed potatoes with homemade gravy type of damn dinner.* Night-Night opened the door to receive the pizza and pay the guy delivering it.

When she cracked the door, she was almost knocked the fuck down by the two men entering behind the fake pizza man. Night-Night screamed loud, but one of the masked men grabbed her ass in a choke hold and placed his hand over her mouth and his gun to her head. The fake pizza man closed the door and locked it. He watched the door.

"Where the fuck is your man, bitch?" the masked man holding her asked.

She didn't say shit.

That's when the other masked man stepped to the bathroom door and heard Capone shout, "Night-Night, c'mere. I need you to massage this shampoo in my scalp for me, baby." The masked man at the bathroom door turned the knob with his Mack 10 fully automatic Uzi in his hand down at his side.

Night-Night was trying to warn Capone of the approaching danger, but her screams were muffled by the strong hand of the masked man who held his hand at her mouth tightly. Night-Night only had on one of Capone's shirts and her panties.

The masked man at the bathroom door entered. He saw Capone with his head underneath the showerhead, massaging his scalp. When Capone looked up and saw the masked man, it was too late for him to make any sudden moves. "You a dead muthafucka!" the masked man barked, with his Mack 10 aimed straight at Capone's chest. Capone was fuckin' speechless.

"Nigga, you beat my cousin into a coma; now you gotta answer for that."

Capone looked behind the masked man and saw another one approaching with Night-Night in his tight grip. "She ain't got nothing to do with this," Capone said. "If y'all want me, then here I am. You got me." He lifted his hands and tried stepping out the shower. The masked man who wasn't holding Night-Night punched Capone straight in his chin, knockin' him backward. He slipped in the tub and busted his ass, nearly breaking his leg. Night-Night saw this and screamed.

The masked man then started beating the hell out of Capone with his gun. Blood splattered everywhere. Capone tried fighting back in spite of his no-win situation, but he kept slippin' in the tub. Night-Night managed to get loose from the masked man who held her by elbowing him in the groin. He folded and watched her jump on the back of the masked man who was now beating Capone damn near unconscious with his gun.

"Get off of him, muthafucka," she said between hitting him with her fists. But her attack was short-lived. He swung her ass off of him.

"Bitch!" he shouted, giving her a hard smack on her jaw with his open palm. His brother then regained his strength from being briefly weakened by Night-Night's blow to his groin. "I got her ass," he said, as he got on top of her. He was meaning to sit on her stomach and put his hand over her neck to choke her ass out. But before he could sit on her stomach, she lifted her legs and started kicking.

"Bitch, be still!" he shouted, punching her in the chin. The punch knocked her out cold. He then looked over and saw his brother with the cord from a nearby hair dryer wrapped around Capone's neck.

"I'ma choke this muthafucka to death. I want his ass to suffer just like our goddamn cousin suffered when he was beating him with his gun," the masked man said to his brother, who was on his knees in front of Night-Night. She and Capone were knocked completely out. "Wake the fuck up, muthafucka," the masked man said to Capone, as he hit him hard as he could with his gun.

Capone came to, only to find himself in a brutal struggle for air. The cord that the masked man had around his neck and was choking him with was utterly depriving him of oxygen. The feeling was like being trapped deep underwater, unable to breathe.

The masked man who was over Night-Night looked her body over as she lay on the floor out cold. Through the 5X T-shirt she had on, the masked man could see that she had some nice big titties. And when he caused his eyes to go farther downward, the see-through fishnet pink panties she was wearing made him want to do something that he had not come there to do: fuck her. He placed both his hands on each side of her waist, pulled her panties down to her ankles, and then lifted her legs. While her legs were lifted over one side of his shoulder, he unzipped his pants and pulled his dick out.

"What the fuck are you doing?" his brother yelled at him. His brother had already strangled Capone.

"I'm 'bout to fuck this bitch," his brother replied. He had his hard dick at the entrance of her vagina.

He was about to thrust it in her, but his brother grabbed him aggressively by the arm. "That's not what we came here for."

"Man, fuck that bitch!" his brother said.

"Looka here, bruh, I'm not gonna let you rape this bitch. Fuck that. Now put your dick back in your pants and let's finish what we came here to do." His brother looked down at Night-Night laid out on the floor with her panties down.

He then looked over at Capone laid out in the tub with the cord of a hair dryer around his neck. His face was purple. There was no doubt his ass was dead from strangulation. He looked back over and down at Night-Night. "Man, look at how pretty her pussy is. I gotta fuck her." When he said that, he saw Night-Night move her leg. She was recovering from being knocked out.

"Ain't no fuckin' going on," his brother assured him, pointing his Mack 10 at her head. He then let go three shots to her face. After he shot and killed her, he sprayed Capone's body up with about five shots. If that wasn't enough, his brother, the one who wanted to rape Night-Night, turned his gun on Capone and shot him ten more times. Capone's body jumped and jerked like it was being electrocuted.

That's when both of them heard the guy who came with them dressed as the pizza man shout, "Man, y'all c'mon before somebody call the cops." Both of them walked from the bathroom like nothing fuckin' happened.

Three days later, after Mooky and Pooky laid Capone and Night-Night to rest for what Capone did to their cousin, their cousin died at Carolina Medical Center. Mooky and Pooky cried hard at their cousin Spanky's funeral, but they returned to Philly relieved to know that their cousin wasn't the only one fuckin' pushing up daisies.

***

When Night-Night's mother and father got the call to come down to the morgue to identify their daughter's body, her mother viewed the holes in her daughter's beautiful face and dropped straight down to her knees, crying hard. "I tried to tell her, Lord Jesus, but she just wouldn't listen," she said through her weeping.

Night-Night's father placed his hand on top of his wife's shoulder and started rubbing up and down. Tears fell from his eyes like a river emptying itself after a heavy rainfall. *I wonder if my wife had been a little more courteous to our daughter and her boyfriend would they still be alive?* He didn't express verbally what he was thinking, because he was too busy trying to comfort his wife. Even so, seeing his only child, his baby girl, laid out on the table, dead, made him want to go and get in touch with some of his old friends from the drug game and put out all inquiries as to who could have done this to her and Capone.

But after months of giving this thought a resting place in his heart and going to church, he concluded that vengeance belonged to God. He also concluded that his daughter was a grown woman. One capable of making her own decisions. She chose to be with a thug as well as to be thuggish. A hard pill for any parent to swallow. But one that could be stomached, knowing that as a parent you did everything in your power to see to it that your child didn't travel the wrong road.

Night-Night's mother, however, wept day in and day out over her deceased daughter. "She just wouldn't listen, Lord. She just wouldn't listen," she would say while weeping.

31

Testifying

Derrick stared at Fat Jerome across the courtroom as he was on the stand. "This coward rat-ass bastard," Fat Jerome uttered to himself as his lawyer questioned Derrick. Fat Jerome's lawyer pointed to his client.

"Mr. Derrick Bellamy," he said, "do you know this man sitting over there in this honorable courtroom?"

Derrick cleared his throat. "Yes, sir, I do," he replied, looking straight at Fat Jerome.

"What's his name, Mr. Bellamy?"

"In the streets, I know him as Fat Jerome."

"And how do you know him?"

"I know him because he and I did business together."

"And what type of business would that be, Mr. Bellamy?"

"We hustled coke together. Well, let me rephrase that. He was frontin' me a kilo a time."

"What do you mean by frontin' you?"

"That means he was giving me coke to sell on consignment."

"Okay, I see. So, my client here was your supplier?"

"Pretty much," replied Derrick.

"How many times would you say he supplied you?"

"Umm, about three times."

"Let's be precise here. Was it three times, or about three times?"

"It was three times."

"All right. Now, these three times that you received these three kilos, did you receive them directly from the hands of my client?"

"No, sir. I would be told where to go pick it up," said Derrick.

"But you never received cocaine at all directly from my client's hands?"

"That's correct," Derrick replied, looking over at Agent Amy Williams and her partner who was sitting up front in the courtroom. Agent Williams winked and smiled.

"If you never received cocaine directly from my client's hands, then how can you honestly say that the cocaine you were receiving belonged to him?"

"I knew that it belonged to him because we would meet and he would tell me from his own mouth where to go pick up the cocaine after I would pay him off."

"But again, he never put any drugs in your hands, right?"

"Right."

"So if you are in fact telling this courtroom the truth, then it would be absolutely no problem at all to look at the jury and say out loud that my client, Mr. Jeremiah Jerome Jenkins, never put drugs in your hands personally."

"Your Honor, I would object to my client doing that," Derrick's attorney stood up and interjected.

Fat Jerome's lawyer shot back, "Your Honor, my client has been dubbed by the prosecuting attorneys as one of the biggest drug dealers in Charlotte, North Carolina. But everyone who has taken the stand against him has failed to prove that they have personally received drugs from his hands. Therefore, I object to Mr. Bellamy's attorney's objection, because the matter involves whether or not my client is who the government claims he is."

"Fair enough. Objection overruled. You may continue," the judge declared.

"Look over at that jury, Mr. Bellamy, and tell them for the record that my client, Mr. Jeremiah Jerome Jenkins, has never placed drugs in your hand." Derrick did as he was told, only because it was the truth. Fat Jerome's lawyer then looked at Derrick. "You have never personally received drugs from my client, yet the government has called you to testify. Tell this courtroom and the jury the real reason you're on the stand testifying."

"What you mean, the real reason?" Derrick repeated.

"What I mean is you were in prison on a gun violation. Am I correct?"

"Yes, sir."

"The FBI and the government offered you an opportunity to get out of prison, provided you agreed to testify against my client. Is that correct?"

"Somewhat."

"Well, it is or it isn't, Mr. Bellamy."

"That's correct. I promised the government that I would provide truthful testimony and they agreed to get me out of prison on those conditions."

"Yet, the truth is you never received drugs personally from my client, correct?"

"Correct."

"Your Honor, that's all I have for right now." Fat Jerome's attorney then walked back to his seat, which was at a table next to Fat Jerome. He gave Fat Jerome a wink as if he had proven Derrick to be a nonthreatening witness. But nothing could've been further from the truth, because the prosecuting attorney for the government stood up with more bullets in the chamber.

"Mr. Bellamy," said the prosecutor, an elderly white man with streaks of gray running through his brown hair. He was also very tall with a clean face. His eyes were bluish green. He removed his clear glasses from his face. "How old are you, sir?"

"I'll be twenty-three December twenty-first."

"Did you graduate high school?"

"Yes, sir."

"You did so with no problem at all, now didn't you?"

"That's correct, sir."

"Then it would be fair enough to say to this here jury that you are not a dumb man by a long shot. I mean, your ability to read, write, and comprehend things is pretty good, correct?"

"I would like to believe so, sir."

"Okay, now how long would you say you were hustling in the streets?"

"About a good year before I was arrested."

"In the streets, where those who break the law have to be on point at nearly all times, how likely is it for someone to put out a hit on someone who has not wronged them at all?"

"That's highly unlikely. No criminal wants unnecessary blood on his hands."

"You informed the government that you received kilos of coke on consignment from Mr. Jeremiah Jenkins, correct?"

"That's correct."

"You also informed the government that you refused to pay Mr. Jenkins for the last kilo of coke that he allowed you to have because he violated a girlfriend of yours, is that correct?"

"Yes, sir, it is."

"Shortly afterward, a hit man was sent to kill you. Correct?"

"Correct."

"Explain that to this jury."

"Like I said earlier, Fat Jerome—I mean, Jeremiah Jenkins—was giving me coke on consignment. I always made sure that he was paid. I would give him directly twenty-five thousand cash. Usually, I would bring the money to his pool hall over in North Charlotte in a brown grocery bag. However, the last time he allowed me a kilo of coke, I refused to pay him. I refused to pay him because my girlfriend at the time had informed me that while at a private party held at his house, he got her pissy drunk and when she awoke the next day at his house, she noticed that she had been sodomized. When she told me that Jeremiah Jenkins over there was the culprit, I was so angry that I literally wanted to kill him. My girlfriend talked me out of carrying that thought out, though. I had to get him back. So, I decided to keep the money I owed him.

"About a month and a half later, I was on my way home one late night and a man eased behind me and put a knife to my throat. Luckily a friend of mine, who is now deceased, was nearby. He placed a gun to this hit man's head and demanded that he remove the knife from my neck. At gunpoint, the hit man not only told us who sent him in exchange for his life, but he also went back and talked Jeremiah Jenkins into paying my ex-girlfriend thirty thousand for violating her."

"Thank you, Mr. Bellamy. Now, with you not being a dummy at all, do you think that Mr. Jeremiah Jerome Jenkins would have sent that hit man to kill you over drugs that did not belong to him?"

"No, sir, I don't."

"Had those drugs not belonged to him person-ally, whether he placed them in your hands or not, your life would not have been in jeopardy, now would it?"

"That is true."

"Your Honor and ladies and gentlemen of the jury, this young man's life was constantly in danger as a result of him refusing to pay up drug money that belonged to Mr. Jenkins over there. That drug money belonged to Mr. Jenkins only because the drugs belonged to him. What indi-vidual would wanna kill another over something that doesn't belong to him? I simply ask the ladies and gentlemen of the jury that you see Mr. Jeremiah Jerome Jenkins for who he really is: a man willing to do any- and everything to keep his drug empire going. If that means murder, so be it. If that means flooding the whole north side with coke and heroine so that your sons and daughters can either use or sell his product, so be it. The man is a drug dealer. A notorious one at that. Someone this city could definitely do without."

The prosecution then sat down. Derrick removed himself from the stand with Fat Jerome giving him a mean-ass stare as if to say, "Son of a bitch, you and that stankin' bitch girlfriend of yours ain't shit. I should have killed the both of y'all my goddamn self!"

Prior to Derrick getting on the stand, Veronda had done so. Her testimony fucked up Fat Jerome, Osama, Ericka, and six other underlings from Fat Jerome's crew. She made Ericka so mad, testifying against her, that Ericka yelled in the courtroom at her while she was on the stand, "Bitch, whatever fuckin' happened to sticking to the rule of keepin' your damn mouth shut? When I get out, your ass is mine. Bitch, I promise you that!"

Veronda didn't even trip at Ericka's sudden outburst. The only thing that was going through Veronda's mind was the fact that what goes around comes back a-fuckin'-round. *That bitch was gonna help Fat Jerome and them niggas kill me, so I had to tell the jury all about all of those kilos of coke and muthafuckin heroine and guns she and I transported up and down the highway for Fat Jerome. Damn right I ratted with no remorse.*

Fat Jerome and every member of his crew received life without parole. The government's main objective was to make an example out of Fat Jerome and his crew. Drug dealers and their notorious way of operating their drug empires would not be taken lightly. Not by the feds or any other branch of law enforcement. They would all work in shifts, if need be, to show that lawbreakers such as Fat Jerome and his crew would be eliminated by all means.

Shortly after the trial was over, Derrick and Veronda started back dating heavy. Derrick moved her in with him, his mom, and Mike-Mike. At first Veronda was hesitant to live with them, but when she saw that they stayed on the outskirts of Charlotte where it was quiet and not in the city, she moved in. Derrick's mom even helped her get a job doing what she was doing, which was housekeeping for the same elderly retired doctor. Derrick finished barber school and copped a chair in a barbershop that was on the east side of Charlotte. A part of Charlotte where he didn't know anybody. The only person his ass knew on that side of town was Agent Amy Williams. She had a condo nearby.

In fact, it was her idea for him to check out the barbershop that was near her place so that if he rented a chair out of that shop, he could be near her and she could get her some of his dick on the low, without him having to travel too far to get to her.

And yes, she and Derrick damn near on a weekly basis were fuckin' the hell out of each other. Derrick knew that he loved the heaven out of Veronda. But he also felt that he was just too damn young to just have one woman in his stable. Having two would suit him fine, as long as he kept the matter secret from Veronda. Veronda was doing good, working. She was very distant from the streets and the mentality that came with them. But sharing her goddamn man with a white FBI agent was something her ass would have put Derrick's ass in check on with the quickness. That's why Derrick and FBI Agent Amy Williams kept their little secret just that. A secret.

Li'l Mike-Mike later graduated and was soon on his way to college. His mother was so happy and so were Derrick and Veronda. Derrick was so happy and proud of Mike-Mike that he summoned him and Veronda to his bedroom and asked Veronda to give Mike-Mike a graduation present. Some head! Veronda dropped straight to her knees and made Mike-Mike's whole body tremble. When it was over, Mike-Mike hugged Derrick with a big smile. "You're the best brother a little brother could ever wish for. Thank you."

ORDER FORM
URBAN BOOKS, LLC
97 N. 18th Street
Wyandanch, NY 11798

Name (please print):_____

Address:_____

City/State:_____

Zip:_____

QTY	TITLES	PRICE

Shipping and handling-add $3.50 for 1st book, then $1.75 for each additional book.
Please send a check payable to:
Urban Books, LLC
Please allow 4-6 weeks for delivery